About the Author

Verily Anderson knows just what is involved in taking a Pack to France for a day! She has raised two Brownie Packs, one in the country and one in London. Since she was ten, she has been active in the Movement as a Guide, Lieutenant, Tawny and Brown Owl. She has worked on the staff of *The Guide* and is a writer for and about Brownies and Guides.

Text copyright © 1964 Verily Anderson
Illustrations copyright © 1964 Brockhampton Press

First published 1964 by Brockhampton Press
This edition Knight Books 1980

Set, printed and bound in Great Britain for
Hodder and Stoughton Paperbacks, a
division of Hodder and Stoughton Ltd,
Mill Road, Dunton Green, Sevenoaks,
Kent (Editorial Office: 47 Bedford
Square, London, WC1 3DP) by
Cox & Wyman Ltd, Reading

ISBN 0 340 191139

Contents

1 · Summery plans

It was a freezingly cold day, with March winds and winter frosts underfoot and even thin ice on the ponds. Most of the Brownies ran all the way to the barn where they had their meeting and arrived with red noses and tingling fingers. Brown Owl had already been there once to light the stove, which made the barn as warm as anybody's own home. Now she came back again with a pile of exciting-looking things to use for games and Brownie work.

'Ooh!' squeaked Trixie, 'I can see some dolls' knives and forks!' And she jumped up and down. 'Perhaps Brown Owl will test me for laying the table today.'

They were taking off their coats and scarves and gloves and hanging them on the pegs. This was usually the time for all the latest gossip.

'Have you heard?' Olivia said. 'Mary and Cherry and Pat are all going up to Guides.'

'That's all our Sixers,' Anne said. 'So all three

Sixes will have to have new ones. I wonder who they'll be.'

'They'll be the Seconds, won't they?' Jeanie said. 'Amanda and Olivia and Tulip.'

Lucinda's cousin, Tulip, said: 'What about Lucinda? She's nearly a Highway Brownie, and she's older than all the others.'

'But she hasn't been in our Pack for long,' Olivia reminded her.

'Twit, twit, twit, twit,' Brown Owl called the Brownies, and they all stopped talking to hurry round Brown Owl and Tawny, who were standing in the middle of the barn. They went through the opening ceremomy, and then had a Pow-wow.

'Now we'll hear who's going to be the new Sixers,' whispered Lucinda, but all the talk to begin with was about what they were going to do in the summer. It seemed a long way away. Through the windows they could see the cold, grey sky with the birds being blown about in it. Underneath her tunic Amanda could feel her winter vest tickling her slightly. And yet here was Brown Owl talking about their Pack Holiday, and all the Brownies who were old enough to have belonged to the Pack last summer started thinking about the sunshine. They thought about the warmth, and bathing in the sea, and lying on the shore, and digging in the sands, and all the lovely things they did in the dream house they had stayed in on the cliffs.

'Will Harry come with us again this year?' Tulip asked.

'We must have Harry!' several of the Brownies chorused together. Harry was Tawny's brother.

'I'm afraid not this year,' Tawny said. 'He's got to work for his exams.'

The Brownies groaned, and it sounded like snow sliding off the roof.

'Where are we going this time?' Tulip wanted to know.

'Well, that's the thing,' said Brown Owl. 'There's something that will have to be rather different this year, and that's the matter of time.'

'We've got the whole of the summer holidays,' Lucinda said.

'We don't mind how long we're away.'

'Our mothers can manage without us.'

'Let's stay away a whole month.'

Everybody talked at once.

'That's just it. We know the Brownies have got lots of lovely time for our Pack Holiday. But unfortunately Tawny and I will only have three days, apart from ordinary Pack meetings,' Brown Owl said.

There was another groan, that this time sounded like slates sliding off the roof.

'Then let's go back to our holiday house for three days,' suggested Cherry.

'One day to get there. One day to be there – and one day to get back.' Brown Owl shook her head. 'It doesn't seem worth it, does it?'

'Yes!' roared all the Brownies. 'We had lots of fun in the train both ways.'

'Tawny and I have another idea, and that includes fun in the train, too. How would you like to go to France for a day?' Brown Owl asked.

Now the sound was not so much like snow falling off the roof. It was more like something gone wrong with the chimneys that made them whistle and shriek, for all the Brownies agreed that a day in France would be the most wonderful thing they could think of.

'But what shall we do with the other days?'
Jeanie asked.

'We'll spend one whole day getting ready
together,' Brown Owl suggested. 'And there'll be
the day in France.'

'*The* day, the Special Day,' Trixie said dreamily.

'And then,' said Brown Owl, 'there'll be the day
after when we'll all think of a way to make other
people happy as a result of our day in France. How
do you think we could do that?'

'Buy rock for old people and give it to them!'
suggested Amanda.

'Go and cheer people up with our adventures!'
suggested Pat.

'Give a French feast for all our friends with the
food we've brought back,' said Tulip, and then
everybody had ideas.

'Teach people French.'

'Give away pebbles we find on the beach.'

'If we've learnt to swim while we're in France,
teach other people's little brothers and sisters to
swim when we get back.'

'Learn to live with other countries.'

Brown Owl thought these were all excellent
ideas.

'But will we have time to do them all?' Pat asked.

'Perhaps we could have a French Day here at the
barn for everybody to come to – mothers and
fathers and brothers and sisters, and uncles and

aunts and anybody who's interested – and then we could pass on our own lovely day in France,' suggested Tawny.

'How about the swimming?' asked Amanda, who had learnt to swim at last summer's Pack Holiday and was very keen.

'That's where Harry comes in,' said Tawny. 'Harry thinks he can fix you up a small swimming-pool next summer in the dell just below the barn.'

'How will the water stay in?' everybody wanted to know.

'He thinks he can borrow a waterproof haystack cover from a farmer. It won't be very deep, but just big enough to do a few strokes in.'

'Will we bring our own water?'

Tawny smiled. 'No, Trixie, I don't think we'd have enough even if everybody brought a mugful!' she said. 'Harry thought that with a little digging he could divert the stream so that it runs into your pool and then overflows to run away the other end.'

'That'll keep the water nice and clean, won't it?' Brown Owl said.

'Will you ask him to make a waterfall, Tawny?' Jeanie asked her.

'And fountains!'

'And a diving-board!'

'And a water-chute!' they suggested.

Brown Owl and Tawny both laughed now.

'Harry isn't magic, you know!' Brown Owl said.

'I think it'll be very clever of him if he can just make a pool.'

'Very clever!' agreed the Brownies.

2 · A new Six called Kelpies

There was so much to talk about. The day of getting ready and what the Brownies would all do on it, and the day in France itself, and then the French day at home. Brown Owl found it quite hard to get everybody started on playing games. There were only three people who were not looking excited end happy – Mary, Cherry and Pat. The three Sixers who were going up to Guides were all looking worried.

They, of course, would not be there for the Special Day.

Half-way through, Brown Owl called them into the little alcove in the barn, where the thin, wintry sun came in palely through the window.

'Cheer up, you three! Don't forget the Guides are going to camp.'

'But will we be allowed to, as we're so new?' Cherry asked.

'You won't be so new then,' Brown Owl said. 'I

happen to know that they are all going to camp in Cornwall this summer.'

'Camping will be lovely,' Mary said with a sigh, 'but I shall miss being a Brownie.'

'We shall miss you all, too,' Brown Owl smiled. 'But of course you'll come to the French Day, won't you?'

'We'll come and help!' Pat offered at once.

'Now let's talk about who'll be the new Sixers when you've gone up to Guides,' Brown Owl said.

'Won't the Seconds take on from us?' Cherry asked. 'They're all Brownies, Amanda, Olivia and Highway Tulip.'

'Yes, they will,' Brown Owl said, 'but several mothers have asked me whether there will be room in the Pack for more Brownies, and I think the time has come to have another Six. As you three have been in the Pack the longest, I thought perhaps you would like to choose its name.'

'We've got Pixies and Elves and Imps ...' Cherry said, 'what else could we have? Fairies and Leprechauns – they're Irish, aren't they? Kelpies – they're Scottish.'

'Can the new Six be Kelpies?' Mary said with a slow grin.

'Yes, do let it be Kelpies!' Cherry and Pat said together.

'Right,' Brown Owl agreed. 'Kelpies it shall be.'

'Who'll be the Sixer?' Pat wanted to know.

'That's what we have to decide,' Brown Owl said.

'Anne's been in the Pack next longest after Amanda, Olivia and Tulip,' Cherry pointed out.

'Lucinda's older,' Pat said.

'Lucinda's been in the Pack shortest of anybody except Trixie,' went on Cherry.

'She was a Brownie in London before,' Mary reminded them.

'But she still skips the wrong way,' said Cherry.

'That wouldn't be very good for a Sixer,' Pat agreed.

'She's trying very hard!' Mary said, 'and she's almost got her Highway badge.'

'Who do you think ought to be the new Sixer, Brown Owl?' Cherry asked.

'I want you to decide,' Brown Owl said. 'I'll leave you to talk it over, and then come and tell me what you think.'

She went to round up the Brownies who were playing a throwing and catching game. When the game was over, Cherry came up to Brown Owl to tell her what the Sixers thought.

'Well,' Brown Owl asked, 'what have you decided?'

'We think,' Cherry said in a low voice, 'as Lucinda's got nicer and nicer, it ought to be her. She'll have such a little time left before she goes up to Guides. The only thing is, if there's going to be a

Scottish Six, Amanda ought to be the Sixer, because she's got a Scottish grandmother and a kilt.'

'All right,' Brown Owl agreed. 'We'll have to have some changing round, anyhow, as we won't want to have a Six of all new Brownies.'

'It'll mean rather a lot of changing of badges for the mothers,' Cherry said.

'Why not for the Brownies?' Brown Owl said. 'Most of you can hem.'

And so, at the end of Brownies that day, Brown Owl told them the other bit of news, that when Mary and Cherry and Pat left to go up to Guides after the Easter holidays, there would be some changes in the Pack. Tulip would be Sixer of the Imps, Olivia Sixer of the Elves, Lucinda Sixer of the Pixies—

Everybody looked anxiously towards Amanda, as though there must have been a mistake. 'And Amanda . . .' Brown Owl said quickly, 'is going to be the Sixer of our new Six, the Kelpies.'

There was a roar of approval because everybody liked Amanda. Then they wanted to know what Kelpies were and the whole Pack wanted to be in the new Six. But Brown Owl and Tawny had already sorted out who was going to be in which Six, and now Brown Owl read out the names of the new Brownies who would be coming next week. Nobody took much notice of these till she came to Sassy's name.

There was a new groan from those who knew Sassy, and then all the Brownies began to talk at once.

'Oh, no. Not the terrible twin!'

'She can't possibly be a Brownie! She's much too naughty!'

'She'd never get clean enough!'

'Or quiet enough. Or polite enough. She'd never come down out of the trees to come to Brownies, and Sammy, her twin, is much worse. He squirts us with waterpistols.'

'So does Sassy!'

'Not even a water-pistol! She took her mother's new washing-up liquid and poured it down the sink and filled the plastic bottle with water and squirted it at us.'

'She couldn't possibly be a Brownie!'

Brown Owl held up her hands to stop the noise.

'Really, Brownies!' she said. 'What a lot of terrible tell-tales! Anybody'd think that you were always good! And polite and clean, and never went up trees!'

'We don't squirt people with our mother's washing-up liquid bottle,' Lucinda said primly.

'She's much too terrible for Brownies,' said Trixie.

'What are Brownies for?' asked Brown Owl. 'There wouldn't be any point if you were all perfect when you joined.'

'We could still have lots of fun and go to France.' Lucinda suggested.

'But how dull it would be,' Brown Owl said. 'Nobody getting better at anything, and everybody perfect! Think how disappointing it would be when the new Brownies come if they already know all about Journeys and Challenges and Ventures and how to help other people.'

'And they're already trying to do their duty to God and save the Queen,' added Mary.

'And they're putting their badges on properly,' added Amanda.

'Oh, yes, it'll be much better if they're all terrible bothers,' Pat agreed.

'Really frightful, and we all have to help them to turn into Brownies!' said Tulip.

3 · *Not much of a recruit*

But the five little girls who turned up in ordinary
clothes for Brownies next week were not at all
frightful. They were very shy and very quiet, and
did what they were told, and all tried very hard to
catch up with the other Brownies and do what they
were doing. Amanda could guess that Brown Owl
was looking round for the big terror, Sassy, the terrible twin – wondering when she was going to
attack or break up the place as she would surely do.

Brown Owl could not possibly have guessed from
the descriptions of the Brownies last week that the
smallest of the recruits, wearing a clean grey skirt
and jersey, neat socks and shoes, who sat in the
Kelpies' corner, was Sassy. Her curly mop of hair
was brushed tidily down and her freckled face was
shining with cleanliness. He blue eyes were alert as
she watched the Pixies act a play which they made
up as they went along to show the new recruits
what the Brownie Law was.

'A Brownie Guide thinks of others before herself and does a good turn every day.'

This was at the beginning of Brownies. It was a lovely day and Brown Owl decided that they could all go down into the glade. They would decide how they could make it even more lovely when the trees were out and Harry made them their swimming-pool. The minute Sassy got out she began to run and shout and turn head-over-heels to make up for the big strain of her first good impression.

'We'll never be able to take her to France,' Lucinda said in a whisper, making her way back to the Brownie barn. 'She'd ruin the day.'

'It's quite a long time before we're going,' Tulip said. 'Perhaps she might be different by then.'

As it was Cherry's and Pat's and Mary's last Brownies, they chose the rest of the games that day. The recruits tried hard to play them properly and everybody helped them along.

'Just think,' Cherry said to Pat and Mary, 'this time next week it will be us who'll be the new recruits, doing everything wrong at Guides.'

'Yes, so soon after being the top people, we'll be completely bottom!'

'Life's like that, I expect,' Mary sighed. 'You keep on starting again.'

Pat looked down at her outgrown Brownie tunic which, all the same, was the biggest tunic in the Pack. 'And to think when we came to Brownies we weren't much bigger than them!' She nodded towards the recruits, tearing in and out of the other Brownies in a last game of 'Arms and Legs'.

On the way back from the Brownie barn Sassy suddenly started to pick up sticks and throw them in the air. After a bit the Brownies saw why. High up in a tree her twin brother Sam (who was almost exactly like her except that his curls were cut shorter) was hurling oakapples down at the Brownies.

'Come on up, Sass, and help me to bomb the others!'

They usually ganged up together against everybody else. Sassy started towards the tree.

'You're not going to Brownies again next week, are you, Sass?' Sam asked her.

'I don't know yet,' Sassy said.

But when it was time for Brownies again next

week, Sassy was there. She had seen all the others going off up the hill and decided to go, too. This time she was not so clean and neat, for her mother had not got her ready.

It was strange feeling having none of the old Sixers any more, and it was odd having four Sixes instead of three, led by Brownies who were still not quite sure what Sixers had to do. The new recruits were not quite sure what they had to do, either. And all this meant that everybody had to do a lot of thinking for each other, helping each other along. The new recruits had to be taught what they had to do for their tests, and what would happen when they were enrolled, and what they would promise to try to do.

Brown Owl was trying to teach Sassy the Promise.

'I promise that I will do my best to do my duty to God, to serve the Queen and help other people, and to keep the Brownie Guide Law,' Sassy repeated after her.

'Do you think you would like to make that promise, Sassy?' Brown Owl asked her.

'Yes,' said Sassy, 'but I don't expect I'll keep it, because I'm never very good. It's being a twin, my mother says.'

'Twins are often very good,' Brown Owl told her. 'You see, they can help each other to remember to be kind and helpful. Single people have to remember on their own.'

Sassy looked very surprised. 'Do you mean Sam could help me to be good?' she asked.

'Yes, and you can help him.'

This seemed a good idea to Sassy, and she thought about it for a little and then said: 'Well, anyway, I could try, couldn't I?'

'That's what you promise to do as a Brownie,' Brown Owl said. 'You promise to try.'

'Oh, that's not so bad,' Sassy said with relief. 'I was thinking we had to promise we *would* be good.'

'It's no good making promises we know we can't keep,' Brown Owl said. 'That's why the Brownie Promise says "*try*".'

When all the work was done, Tawny suggested that they should play a game in French to start getting ready for the day in France in the summer. Brown Owl and Tawny had written the names in French on lots of pieces of paper of all sorts of things they might want to buy. Beside the names Tawny had drawn, in her own funny way, pictures to match. All the Brownies lined up and each took a piece of paper, and then looked to see what they had got. They asked Brown Owl or Tawny how to say the word, because the same word was said differently in English. Soon everybody was practising their own words and there was quite a hub-bub of French – or sort-of-French.

'Now we'll go shopping,' said Brown Owl, and she pretended to be the shop person, and each Brownie in turn came to buy what was on her piece of paper. Of course the Brownies had to say 'Please' and 'Thank you' ('*S'il vous plaît*' and '*Merci*') and some of the Brownies then took it in turns to be shop people and they all had different pieces of paper.

'Will we have to have passports, Brown Owl, on the day?' Olivia asked her.

'No, we're going to have special tickets that take us to Dieppe just for the day.'

'Will we have to start very early in the morning?'

'Very early,' said Brown Owl. 'We shall all meet at the station at seven and eat our breakfast in the train. Then we go to Newhaven and get on to our boat.'

'Will it take long?'

'Several hours,' said Brown Owl, 'but we'll arrive in France in time for lunch.'

'Will it be dark when we get home?'

'Yes, it will be quite dark.'

'Can my brother Sam come, too?' Sassy asked.

'I'm afraid not, Sassy. This is going to be the Brownies' own special summer holiday, but he can come to our French Day after we get back.'

'I think he'd rather come to France,' Sassy persisted.

'Our French Day will be so like France,' Jeanie said, 'that he won't be able to tell the difference.'

'Last year we made pinafores to wear on our Pack holiday, didn't we, Brown Owl?' Tulip reminded her. 'Can we start making something now for our day abroad?'

'I was thinking about that,' said Brown Owl. 'What do you think we'll need?'

'We'll each need a picnic-bag,' suggested Tulip.

'And we'll need a first-aid kit; one for each Six. And we'll need bags for collecting shells and the things we buy in France,' said Amanda.

'Can we make our picnic-bags, Brown Owl?' Olivia asked.

'All right,' said Brown Owl, 'and each Six shall make its own bags for food, and for things you pick up on the shore and for shopping.'

Next week Harry came at the end of Brownies and all the Brownies helped him to dig a new bed for the stream, so that it would run into the swimming-pool he was going to make them. There was a lot of work to be done in the dell to make it into a nice place for the French Day. Bramble shoots had to be cut down and paths made to start with.

'It's a pity we haven't got anything to line the paths with,' Olivia said.

'We shall have, after the French Day,' Tulip reminded her. 'We'll have shells.'

Every week the Brownies did something towards getting ready for their day abroad and the day after at home. Almost before they had noticed it, the cold spring was behind them and the summer had come. Enrolment day was settled, and all the mothers and the recruits who were going to be enrolled as Brownies were asked to come to tea, and so were younger brothers and sisters.

'But what about my brother?' Sassy asked Brown Owl anxiously. 'He isn't younger, he's exactly the same age as me.'

'Yes, he can come, too,' Brown Owl said.

'When are we going to have our Brownie tunics?' Sassy wanted to know.

'I'm coming to see all your mothers today after Brownies, and I am going to bring the uniforms with me,' Brown Owl promised her.

All the recruits were very pleased to hear this. They had all been measured when they first came, and now they were sure they would have all grown out of their uniforms in the six weeks they had been coming to Brownies.

'It's such a terrible long time, Brown Owl,' Sassy

said. 'Why can't Brownies just be Brownies at once?'

'There are quite a lot of things they have to learn before they can go about the world showing what a Brownie is,' Brown Owl explained. 'Anyone who hadn't learnt them and hadn't made her promise, who put on uniform, would just be someone dressed up as a Brownie – not the real thing at all.'

'I'm longing to be the real thing,' said Sassy.

Five minutes later she had forgotten about her longing. She was pulling all the coats off the pegs to tease Amanda.

'Quickly, Sassy! Help me to pick them all up again!' said Amanda.

Sassy only rolled on them and then pulled the coats on top of her, laughing and giggling and being no help at all. Some of the other Brownies went to help Amanda to hang the coats up again.

'Brown Owl won't let Sassy be enrolled if she's as naughty as this,' Lucinda said.

'But she must be enrolled,' said Amanda. 'It would be terrible if we were the only Six without a recruit at the enrolment. Commissioner's coming specially.'

Amanda tried to explain all this to Sassy, but she only ran round in circles, laughing. Poor Amanda looked really worried. 'What can I do with her?' she asked the other Sixers.

'Try talking to Sam,' Tulip suggested. 'He's the

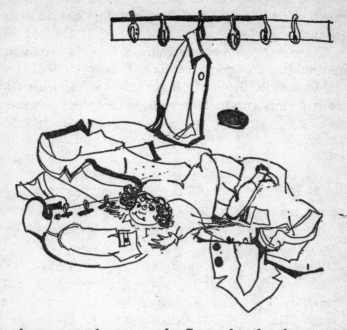

only person who can make Sassy do what he wants
once she starts being naughty.'

'The trouble is, the things he makes her do are
usually even naughtier than her own ideas,' said
Olivia.

'I'll try talking to Sam,' said Amanda.

After Brownies, on the way home, they reached
the place where they usually parted at the cross-
roads, but instead of going across the fields to the
farm where she lived, Amanda set off to look for
Sam. Sassy had told her that he was somewhere

down by the river, but she would not come and look for him.

'Perhaps,' thought Amanda, 'because she's guessed that I'm going to talk to him about her.'

Meanwhile Brown Owl got into her car with all the new uniforms to drive round to see the mothers.

4 · *Amanda talks to Sam*

Amanda found Sam in a willow tree overhanging a muddy part of the river. As soon as he saw her he mysteriously disappeared. Amanda went on along the towpath, and when she got nearer she saw that the upper part of the tree was hollow like a chimney, with an opening half-way up the tree like a fire-place. She could just see Sam squinting out from his hiding-place.

'Hallo, Sam!' she called up to him.

Sam whistled back at her rudely.

'Can I come and talk to you?'

Sam's cheeky face looked out at her. 'If you can swim, you may,' he said.

'I'll paddle,' Amanda said, taking off her shoes and socks and leaving them on the path. It was only floods she had to walk through, not river. She reached the foot of the tree. 'Can I come up?' she asked.

'If you can fly,' Sam said.

'I don't need to fly,' she said. 'I can climb.' And she reached up, caught hold of a branch and swung herself up to it and then crawled along the slanting trunk till she got to the top of the chimney. She looked in. There was Sam, crouching just below her, looking up at her now.

'What do you want to talk about?' he asked.

'Sassy,' she said, easing herself on to another branch and sitting astride it. 'She wants to be a Brownie.'

'No, she doesn't,' said Sam. 'She just says she does to trick you. She's not really going to be a Brownie.'

'Don't you want her to be, Sam?' Amanda asked.

'Me? I don't care what she does. I just know she doesn't want to be one.'

'The thing is,' said Amanda, 'she may not be allowed to be one if she isn't a bit more helpful.'

'What do you mean,' Sam asked, 'not being helpful?'

'Well, doing silly things like pulling all the coats down and then rolling on them and not picking them up,' Amanda said. It didn't sound so unhelpful now as it had when Sassy did it.

'That's nothing. I do much worse things than that. I put a bottle of ink on a door to fall on teacher.'

'And did it?' Amanda asked.

'No, but next time I shall put a bucket,' said Sam

proudly. 'I don't call pulling coats down very bad.'

'Who wants to be bad anyway?' Amanda asked.

'Sassy does. She knows that if she's bad they can't make her a Brownie. If she's good, they'll have to.'

'Not if she doesn't want to be a Brownie. She doesn't have to be one unless she wants to be.'

'They tell her that if she's a Brownie they'll take her to France,' Sam said. 'Just to make her join.'

'We *are* going to France,' Amanda said. 'It's going to be our day abroad in the summer.'

'Do you believe that, too?' Sam said. 'Of course they won't really! It's just to make you go to the meetings. How could anyone take kids all that way? It's just a lot of make-up. You'll see. They'll take you down to the bottom of the wood and say "This is France".'

'That's what we're going to do when we get back from France,' Amanda tried to explain. 'There's a kind of party to share it with all the people who aren't Brownies and can't come.'

'That's all it ever will be,' said Sam. 'You'll see.'

'Well, we're going to France all right,' Amanda assured him.

'Sassy's not!' said Sam. 'I won't let her – if I can't go!'

'I thought twins always helped each other,' Amanda said thoughtfully.

'Twins help each other when they have to,' said Sam, starting to climb out of the chimney. 'Do you want to see how I go fishing?' he asked, changing the subject.

'All right,' said Amanda. It was no use talking to Sam about Sassy. Sam crawled along the branch just above Amanda, and she noticed that he had a fishing-line attached to it. He began to unwind it.

'I let this down,' he said, 'bait it and make it ready, and the fish come along and take it and then I pull them up.'

'Have you caught any?' Amanda asked him.

'Not yet, but I'm going to catch thousands.'

He stood up on the branch and Amanda wished he wouldn't. He was worse than Sassy when he got up a tree. Amanda found climbing trees rather difficult and frightening, but the twins seemed to be just as steady up a tree as they were on the ground.

'Can you swim?' Amanda asked Sam, as she looked down at the water swirling by underneath him.

'I don't need to, anyway, the water's much too cold.'

Amanda agreed. The water looked cold and black and deep. She gave a shiver.

'You can come and have a cup of tea with us, if you like,' Sam said.

Amanda smiled. Perhaps Sam was not quite such a bad boy after all. 'Thank you,' she said, and they set off along the tow-path.

The twins lived not far from the river. Amanda

knew that they had a lot of brothers and sisters, but not that they had so many as she discovered when Sam led the way into the kitchen. There were children of all sizes sitting round the table or strapped into high chairs, or kicking in baskets. At first she did not recognise Sassy among them, because they all looked rather alike, with curly hair and blue eyes. The twins' mother was quite small; she was not much bigger than some of the elder boys.

When she saw Sam she just sighed.

'And I suppose the little girl's someone you have

been leading into mischief, too?' she said of Amanda.

'No,' said Sam. 'I've just brought her home for a cup of tea.'

Sassy suddenly recognised Amanda. She hopped up excitedly and came round to greet her. 'It's Amanda, my Sixer.'

The babies were shouting or cooing or crying, and the small children were beating their spoons on the table, and the older ones were rushing round, and Amanda stood looking on, thinking how nice they were.

'Will you sit by me?' Sassy asked Amanda, making room for her. Sam pushed some of the younger children up and sat down on the bench with them, and then snatched some bread and butter for himself. Amanda soon felt warmer. It was a very jolly tea-party, but the noise was deafening, and most of the children ate straight off the plates in the middle of the table, and took no notice of their own plates, if they had any.

And suddenly, who should come in but Brown Owl! She had brought Sassy's new Brownie uniform. Sassy jumped up again and rushed to the door.

'It's my lovely new Brownie frock!' she exclaimed, 'and my Brown Owl. And look, Brown Owl, Amanda's here!'

Brown Owl was busy with Sassy's uniform.

'Now, Sassy,' she said, 'would you like to try on this tunic? If it's too small I'll change it for another one.'

'Oh, yes,' Sassy said, beginning to get undressed at once. The tunic was not too small; it was much too big. The sleeves hung down over her hands and the hem nearly reached her ankles.

'Oh, dear,' Brown Owl said, 'and it's the smallest size we've got.'

'She just won't grow,' the twins' mother said (and Amanda thought she was going to add, 'I'm always telling her she must, but she won't'), 'but never mind,' she went on, 'we'll just have to put some tucks in it and then it will last all the longer.'

Amanda looked round at all the work the twins' mother would have to do to get all the children to bed before she even began to cook her husband's evening meal. How would she have time to put tucks in Sassy's uniform as well as all that?

'Shall I make the tucks, as I'm Sassy's Sixer?' Amanda offered.

'That's a good idea,' said Brown Owl. 'Tucks in the sleeves and a great big hem at the bottom! You've learnt hemming at school, haven't you?'

Amanda nodded.

'Oh, dear,' said the twins' mother, 'I wish one of my elder ones was a girl! The boys are all right for sawing firewood or anything like that, but if only they could sew!'

'Well, it won't be long before Sassy'll be able to help you,' Brown Owl said.

'Sassy doesn't help at all!' the twins' mother said. 'I only wish she would. And nor does Sam. They're just a couple of terrors!'

Sam and Sassy threw bread at each other to show how terrible they were.

'I've got to go past your farm, Amanda. Shall I give you a lift home?' Brown Owl said, changing the subject.

'Thank you,' Amanda said.

Brown Owl and Amanda said good-bye and got into the car.

'I wish I had lots of little baby brothers and sisters like that to look after!' Amanda said, as they left. 'They really are so sweet. Better then the piglets and the baby chickens, even.'

They reached the farm, and Amanda's mother was just coming out to see whether she could see Amanda returning from Brownies as she was so late.

'Thank you for the lift,' said Amanda.

'Goodbye, and see you at the enrolment,' Brown Owl said as she drove off.

5 · Enrolment in a garden

The enrolment was to be held at Brown Owl's house, so that the Brownies could make tea in her kitchen to give to the mothers and the little brothers and sisters. As her house was near the village, it was much easier for mothers with prams to come there than to push the prams up through the woods to the Brownie Barn.

It was a lovely day. Brown Owl's garden was full of tulips and forget-me-nots and wall-flowers that smelled lovely. There were bees buzzing about and the lawn had just been mown and was smooth and green. The Brownies all went there early to get ready for Commissioner, who had been invited to the meeting.

Only the Sixers were allowed in the kitchen.

Tulip spread the bread and butter and Lucinda put out the cakes, while Olivia and Amanda got out the cups and saucers. The rest of the Brownies were out in the garden putting up the garden tables that

Brown Owl said they could use. She gave them table-cloths and told them where they could find chairs. Jeanie and Trixie decided that there ought to be some flowers on the tables.

'I'll pick them,' said Sassy, and snatched three beautiful tulip heads from the flower-beds with stalks only a few inches long. Jeanie and Trixie gasped. 'You mustn't pick those, Sassy!' Jeanie said. 'They belong to Brown Owl.'

'You said you wanted flowers,' said Sassy, throwing them crossly on the grass.

'Not those sort of flowers. Flowers out of the fields,' Trixie said. 'Oh, dear! What will Brown Owl say! You'd better go and tell her you're sorry, and that you picked them by mistake,' she advised Sassy.

But Sassy would do nothing of the sort. 'If Brown Owl's going to be cross, I'll hide the flowers,' she said, and she took the tulips and threw them away behind the rose-bush.

'Now they'll die,' said Trixie. 'Shall we tell Brown Owl?'

'That'll be telling tales,' said Jeanie. 'It's Sassy who will have to tell Brown Owl.' But when Brown Owl came out, Sassy only ran away.

'Please, Brown Owl, may Trixie and I go and pick some wild flowers to put on the tables?' Jeanie asked.

'What a lovely idea!' said Brown Owl. 'Yes, you

go and pick them and then we'll find some little pots
to put them in. Why don't you go, too, Sassy?' she
said, as Sassy had come out from behind a big lilac
bush where she was hiding.

'I want to stay here,' said Sassy.

'All right,' said Brown Owl, 'but don't run on the
flower-beds, and don't climb the trees. You look so
smart in your new uniform that everybody will be
looking at you when you're enrolled, so you mustn't
get it all dirty before they even arrive.'

Jeanie and Trixie went off to a near-by bank and
picked some lovely bunches of bluebells and red
campions and brought them back to Brown Owl.
Brown Owl gave the Brownies some jars and told
them where they would find a tap in the back-yard
to fill them with water. They arranged the flowers
and put the jars on the tables, which helped to keep

the table-cloths from blowing away before the rest
of the Brownies came along with plates and saucers
to weigh them down at the corners.

There was such a hurry and scurry that no one
noticed that Sassy had disappeared. Then the
mothers began to arrive and with them was the
twins' mother with a big pram full of babies and
several small children toddling along beside it.
Sam, in a white shirt and clean shorts, white socks
and shiny shoes, walked behind them, looking as
good as a little boy out of a painting-book picture.

All the other recruits had met their mothers, but
the twins' mother had no one to meet her. Amanda
saw her wondering what to do and ran over to help
her to get the pram on to the grass and to find
somewhere to sit.

'Don't they all look adorable!' Amanda said, as
she looked into the pram of clean and smiling
babies in their freshly washed and ironed summer
coats and frocks. 'It must have been awfully hard
to get them ready.'

'Yes, I hoped Sassy would help me to get them
ready,' the twins' mother said, 'but she rushed off
before I'd even begun. I suppose she turned up here
all right?' She looked round.

'Oh yes, she's here,' Amanda said. 'I think she
must be helping some of the Brownies with the
dressing-up clothes. We're going to act you a play
after tea.'

There was a 'Twit, twit, twit, twit,' from Brown Owl and Amanda ran off to answer it. Brown Owl was standing at the kitchen door.

'Commissioner will be arriving soon,' she told them, 'and I know she'd like you to meet her at the gate, so will you all run down there now, while I go and say "Hello" to the mothers? But just let me have a last look at the recruits,' she added, 'to make sure that they've put their new uniforms on right.'

'Sassy's not here!' somebody said.

'I don't suppose she's far away. Off you go to the gate,' said Brown Owl, and the Brownies scampered off to the gate, while Brown Owl called Sassy. But there was no answer, and she had to go and say 'Hello' to the mothers and to tell them all about the enrolment, and about the Brownies' day abroad and the French Day.

The mothers had already heard about them both from the Brownies and thought they were wonderful ideas.

'They enjoyed the Pack Holiday so much last year – it's a pity you can't take them to France for a week,' one mother suggested.

'That would be too difficult,' said Brown Owl, 'and too expensive, I'm afraid. We've just got enough in the Pack funds for a day, if you can all subscribe something towards the journey.'

'Of course!' chorused the mothers.

Down by the gate all the Brownies except Sassy were getting ready for Commissioner.

'Let's make her a bridge with our hands!'

'If we all line up we can make make her a tunnel to go through.'

'And let's throw leaves on her and shout and sing.'

'And cover up her car with flowers and things.'

They all rushed to the hedges and picked handfuls of leaves and grass and cow parsley.

They had only just got back to the gate when Commissioner's car came down the lane. She stopped and, as she got out, they rushed towards her, throwing everything they'd picked at her like confetti, and lots over the car as well.

'Hooray – Hooray for Commissioner!'

'Hello! Welcome!' they all roared. Then they dashed back through the gate and formed up in two lines with hands clasped up as high as they could hold them. Commissioner knew what she was supposed to do and bent down to make her way through the tunnel. When she had done this, they all broke away to crowd round her and tell her what the Pack had been doing since she last came to visit them. The recruits, who hadn't met her before, were a little bit shy.

'There are five altogether,' Lucinda told her, 'but one's got lost.'

'Oh, dear, not badly I hope,' said Commissioner.

And suddenly they looked up and there was Sassy, walking along the high wall that divided the flower-garden from vegetables.

Amanda ran over to her. 'It doesn't matter me

being up here,' said Sassy. 'Brown Owl only said I mustn't climb trees.'

'But Brown Owl's been calling you,' Amanda said.

'I wasn't here. I was in the wood getting some flowers like the others did, for the pots,' she said.

'Well, come on now,' said Amanda, 'the enrolment's just going to begin.'

Suddenly Sassy gave a leap. She jumped right over the flower-beds and landed on the grass.

'Now you've got green on your socks from the lawn,' Amanda pointed out.

'How can I get it out?' Sassy asked her.

'You can't,' said Amanda, 'it stains. You'll just have to come as you are.'

They ran across the lawn together to the spot where the toadstool was already standing with the owl on it. Brown Owl had 'twit-twitted' the Brownies round her and Commissioner. All the mothers were watching with interest. The enrolment began and four of the recruits were enrolled. Sassy was the last. Amanda hung tightly on to her hand, afraid that she might rush off at the last minute. She was not worried that Sassy might not know her Promise. It was more that she might spoil the ceremony by doing a cart-wheel or standing on her head. But Sassy did neither. She was good and quiet and solemn, and let Amanda lead her up to Brown Owl to make her Promise. She gave the Brownie salute and her badge was pinned on her tie.

Amanda sighed with relief. Now Sassy really was a Brownie.

The ceremony ended and Brown Owl said that it was time for them to have tea.

When everything was cleared away, the little brothers and sisters had all jumped and rolled on the grass until they were quite tired. When they had returned to their mother's knees, the Brownies acted some plays, showing the kind of thing that Brownies learn to do to help other people. There was just one more play to act and they were all back on the stage (which was the lawn), when they saw three Guides creep in at the back and sit down.

'It's Cherry and Mary and Pat!' Tulip whispered. 'And look, they're completely enrolled, too!'

And so they were, with shining Guide Tenderfoot badges on their ties. The last play was one that they had invented when they were Brownies, and Brown Owl liked it so much that she had said it must always be acted at enrolments.

When the enrolment party was over, everybody went home with their mothers except the Sixers, who stayed behind to make sure that everything was exactly as they had found it. Brown Owl's mother came into the kitchen and said it was perfect. They had washed out the tea-cloths and hung them up to dry.

'You will come to our French Day, won't you?' Tulip asked her.

'I'd love to,' she said, 'but I'm not sure that I shall want to learn to swim. I think I'd rather learn French.'

6 · Stolen jumble

Next week all the Brownies who had just been enrolled were able to join in with everything, and now the Pack was bigger than it had ever been.

'The Brownies' day abroad may cost a bit more then we had thought,' Brown Owl told them. 'And not all the Brownies' mothers can pay towards the journey.'

'Mine can't,' said Sassy. 'She said she couldn't.'

'And then we want to buy some things for our French Day when we get back,' said Brown Owl. 'So the next thing we'll have to do is to make some money. It wouldn't be very Brownie-like just to make money for ourselves to have a lovely time, would it?'

'Some of it would be for the French Day for other people,' Lucinda said.

'Yes, but I think we ought to help other people as well – who do you think needs help?'

'Old people.'

'Babies.'

'Blind people.'

'Lame people.'

'Ill dogs.'

'Poor people's broken-down fences.'

'Yes,' said Brown Owl. 'A lot of people need help, and how do you think we should make some money?'

'Last year we sold tickets for our concert,' Tulip said.

'That was in the winter,' Tawny said. 'Now it's summer – people want to be out of doors more.'

'Let's have an out-of-doors Jumble Sale!' suggested Olivia.

'All right,' said Brown Owl. 'Then you Brownies'll have to collect the jumble and bring it here to the Brownie Barn.'

'And let's have a Lucky Dip at it!' Tulip said.

'A lucky Jumble Dip!' suggested Jeanie.

So the Brownies decided to have an Out-of-Doors Jumble Sale quite soon outside the Brownie Barn, and most of them started collecting jumble for it that very day.

It was surprising how glad people were to get rid of some of the stuff that was taking up too much room in their houses! The Kelpies even collected an old bicycle with a side-car.

The Brownies piled the other things they had collected into the side-car, but by then it was too heavy for any of them to ride. They collected smart hats, and teapots without lids, and – luckily – a lid without a teapot. They collected books and shoes and children's clothes that were too small for them.

On the path up to the Brownie Barn, they met the Elves, carrying their jumble in baskets. They were very interested in what the Kelpies had collected, because they only had children's old clothes and hats.

'A bicycle with a side-car must be worth an awful lot: I wonder who will buy it?' said Tulip.

Brown Owl and Tawny were very pleased with the jumble, and they decided they could have the Jumble Sale within a fortnight. That would give them time to make some big notices for important places telling people where the Jumble Sale would be. It would also give them time to wrap up the smaller things for the Lucky Dip at Brownies next week.

After that first visit, Amanda quite often went to tea with Sassy's family. She would take some of the smaller children into the garden and play with them, but Sassy and Sam would never play. They preferred to go up the trees surrounding the garden and throw things down on to the babies on the grass underneath.

'Why don't you come down, both of you, and play properly with the others?' Amanda asked one

evening. 'It's the silliest game in the world, and look
how you're spoiling the tree! You've broken off so
many bits and pieces to throw at the babies that
there's hardly anything left of it.'

'Who cares?' said Sam rudely.

'It's only a silly old tree, anyway,' said Sassy,
even more rudely.

'It would have had apples on it,' said Amanda,
'but it won't be able to now.'

Sassy and Sam wandered off.

It was lovely looking after the babies without the
twins. None of them cried, and when their mother
had finished the ironing, she came out and sat in the
sun for a little while.

'I was hoping that now Sassy's a Brownie she
wouldn't be so naughty,' her mother told Amanda.

'I'm sure she'll get better soon,' Amanda said
hopefully.

'Well, she does try a bit more,' her mother said,
'and that's something. Oh, well, it's time I took
some of these children away to bed.'

'Can I help you?' Amanda asked.

'Well, if it doesn't make you too late home, yes,' their mother said. So Amanda helped to bath the babies and put them to bed, and then it was time to go home.

The twins had not returned. Amanda wondered wherever they had got to; probably they had been climbing trees.

Next week most of the Brownies arrived at the Barn before Brown Owl. All the jumble was piled up at one end, and the Brownies rushed in to admire it.

As soon as Amanda was inside the Barn she saw that the bicycle with the side-car had disappeared.

'Do you know anything about it?' she asked Sassy.

Sassy shook her head.

'Are you sure?' Amanda asked her.

Sassy shook her head again.

'Then somebody must have stolen it. The Barn was only unlocked for about half an hour one evening for people to bring last-minute jumble, and somebody must have taken it away.'

Suddenly Amanda had a horrible idea. Could Sammy have stolen it? 'Sassy,' she asked, 'are you *sure* you didn't come near the barn the other evening?'

But Sassy would not answer, and Amanda was sure that she was right about Sam.

Before Brownies had ended, Sassy said to Amanda:

'I think Sam will put it back.'

'So Sam *did* take it?'

'I'm sure he'll put it back,' was all Sassy would say.

Next day Amanda went to the Brownie hut with Olivia and peeped in through the window. There was still no bike, and it had not been left anywhere near the Brownie Barn, either.

'I think Sam is a horrid little boy,' Olivia said. 'It's the best thing of all our jumble, and it'll make the most money.'

Then Amanda had an idea. There was a hay-stack quite a long way from the twins' house and she had often seen the twins playing there. They liked to climb up on to the top and then slide down one side. So far the farmer had not discovered how much of the hay was pulled out by the sliding. Amanda decided they had better go and look there for the bicycle.

At first there was no sign of anything unusual. Then they saw a pile of loose hay that looked as if it might be covering something up. They pulled off the hay and underneath was the bicycle with the side-car.

They uncovered it and pulled and pushed and heaved until they got it out into the field, and then it was quite hard work to bump it over the field on to the lane. It was so heavy that they both had to keep pushing all the time, though when they came to a little bit of downhill Amanda got on and rode. Then it was uphill again to the Barn and they had to push harder than ever.

Amanda got the key and unlocked the Barn and they heaved the bicycle up the step and put it with the other things.

'Now we must make sure that we lock everything up very well tonight,' Olivia said.

'And we must cover up the best things so that anyone looking in through the windows can't see them,' said Amanda.

So they got all the clothes and curtains and a big straw mat and put them over the bicycle and the side-car, and underneath they put important things like clocks and pictures and anything specially valuable.

Then they went out and Amanda locked the door.

'I do hope the things'll be safe till the Jumble Sale on Saturday,' Olivia said, giving it one last look.

7 · Harry's home-made pool

After all, when Saturday came, the Sale could not be held out of doors, because it poured with rain all day. Amanda had to look for her Wellingtons that she hadn't worn since the winter, because the puddles were so deep when she started out. She put on her macintosh and scarf tied over the top of her Brownie beret.

There was usually plenty of room in the Brownie Barn for ordinary Pack meetings, but it was going to be rather a squeeze with the stalls for the jumble as well as all the people. The Brownies had spent the morning arranging the things on the stalls and setting up the Lucky Dip. Olivia, who was rather good at drawing and lettering, wrote notices for the stalls: 'THINGS FOR THE DRAWING-ROOM' – 'FILL UP YOUR KITCHEN!' – 'BEDTIME IN COMFORT' – 'FOR THE LUCKY GARDENER!' – and, for things that would not come under any of these titles, there was 'THE BETTER-THAN-NEW STALL'.

Everybody went home for lunch and then came back looking extra clean and neat. It was exciting to see the stream of people coming along the path with their umbrellas up. Brown Owl had to open the Sale by just opening both doors, as there was no grand person to make a speech. Some of the Brownies took the people's umbrellas as they came in and shook them out for them, and others took their macintoshes and hung them on the pegs with their own, promising that they would not be sold. The rest of the Brownies stood behind the stalls with Brown Owl and Tawny, and tin boxes to take the money in.

In no time at all the toys had been sold and most of the books. Most of the clothes disappeared, too, and the stalls got barer and barer. Then Brown Owl said that everything could be made cheaper, and at that moment Amanda saw Sam standing by the bicycle with the side-car which had been marked at the beginning 'One pound fifty'.

'How much shall we make the bicycle, Brown Owl?' Amanda asked.

'Make it fifty pence now,' suggested Brown Owl.

So Amanda made it fifty pence. But still nobody even bothered to look at it, except Sam, and he never took his eyes off it.

'Make it twenty-five pence,' said Brown Owl, and Olivia wrote a special 'Twenty-five pence', with 'BARGAIN' underneath.

'How dreadful if we only get so little for such a lovely thing,' Lucinda said. But still nobody took any notice at all.

Brown Owl came along. 'We simply must get rid of the bicycle. We can't give it back to the people who gave it to us, and I can't think what to do with it.' She saw Sam looking longingly at it, and she whispered to Amanda: 'Put it down to ten pence, and then perhaps Sam will buy it. I can see he wants it, though he's much too small to ride it.'

'Oh, no, Brown Owl, Sam mustn't have it!' Lucinda, who had heard what Brown Owl had said, interrupted.

'Why not?' said Brown Owl.

'Because, and because . . .'

'It's nothing, Brown Owl,' Amanda said quickly. 'He does want it very much, but he hasn't got ten pence, I know.'

'Make it five pence, then,' said Brown Owl.

'He hasn't even got five pence,' Lucinda said, and just then Sassy appeared with some special kitchen gadgets that she had bought. Now she held them up to Brown Owl and said:

'Please, Brown Owl, will you buy these back, so I can buy Sam the bicycle with the side-car?'

Brown Owl looked at Sassy and smiled. 'How sweet of you, Sassy! But I couldn't bear to buy them back, because I know you wanted them so much.'

'Yes, Brown Owl, please do,' Sassy begged her. 'I'd much rather Sam had the bicycle.'

'All right, Sassy,' said Brown Owl, 'if that's what you really want.'

Sam's face lit up, and he looked for one moment like an angel. 'I had a good look at the things,' he told Sassy. 'I saw how things for grating carrots and making potatoes into funny shapes were made, and I can easily make some for you out of the bits left over when I take the bicycle to pieces, but I don't know if I can make those wooden things for rolling butter.'

There was a mixture of pride and sadness on Sassy's face at parting with the gadgets. Brown Owl put them on a stall and watched them carefully, but nobody came to the stall and very soon she was able to say to Sassy:

'Look, Sassy, these things haven't been sold. We can't throw them away, so you'd better take them home after all.'

Now it was Sassy who looked like an angel. 'Oh, Brown Owl, you're so kind!' she cried. 'I've not been nearly good enough for it, but I'll try, and try, and try. Sammy doesn't deserve the bicycle. He's a very naughty boy, and it was very naughty of us to steal it before—'

'Steal it before . . .?' Brown Owl asked.

'We know all about it,' Lucinda said.

'It wasn't really stealing,' said Olivia. 'It was more taking away.'

'It wasn't taking away, it was stealing,' said Sassy. 'But Sam's very sorry, and now he's very glad.'

They could just see him through the window, clattering down the path on the great big bicycle with the side-car attached to it.

'I really am very surprised,' said Olivia, 'that the best thing of all didn't sell.'

'Well it did in the end,' said Tulip.

'If you count Sassy giving back the gadgets,' said Amanda.

'Oh, well, anyway,' said Tawny, 'I haven't counted all the money yet, but I think there'll be plenty for all the people you want to help and some for France as well.'

The next thing was to help Harry to make the haystack cover into a swimming-pool. Everybody wore jeans for this muddy job, even Harry. He spread the big blue cover on the ground and then he told the Brownies to stand round it and pick up and walk with it to the dell. This was where the stream would come when they had dug a channel to make it change its course.

'Come on, Brownies, let it down gently,' Harry said, and Brown Owl and Tawny joined in so that the big plastic sheet should fit as well as possible. It was like laying a giant handkerchief in a shallow bowl.

'And now for the last bit of digging!' said Harry. 'And as I don't want my feet chopped off, I think I'll do it myself.' For the Brownies had all rushed eagerly forward with spades to do it for him. Now they all clustered round him.

'The water's coming itself!'

'It'll push the earth down!'

'Mind out, Harry! Don't let earthy water go into our pool and spoil it!'

'Here it comes!'

'Watch the last dig!'

'Hurray!' they all roared as the little stream rushed in a bubbling waterfall into the new pool. The Brownies stood round with their bare toes curling in the mud as they watched their pool getting deeper and deeper. Soon it was as deep as Olivia's waist, and Olivia was the tallest Brownie in the Pack.

'There's plenty of water there for a few strokes of swimming,' Brown Owl said.

And now the pool began to overflow and make

another waterfall as it splashed back into its old course.

'When are we going to swim in it, Brown Owl?' asked Tulip.

Brown Owl looked at the sky. There were no clouds. The sun was shining brightly and it was really quite warm. 'What about today?' Brown Owl asked. 'Would you all like to get your bathing things and come back this afternoon?'

There was a squeaky roar of joy, and some of the smaller Brownies started to scamper off right away, but Brown Owl called them back. 'No, it's not ready yet,' Brown Owl said.

'And I'll have to get my bathing things so that I can rescue you all,' said Harry.

'If we go on having nice weather like this,' said Brown Owl, 'you'll all be able to swim, even the newest Brownies, by the time we go to France. And then on the French Day you'll be able to teach the little brothers and sisters.'

Every single Brownie turned up that afternoon with a towel and bathing-suit. Brown Owl and Tawny and Harry were there, but Harry was only teasing them when he said that he was going to wear his bathing things, too. It was not deep enough for Harry.

'Let's all jump in together!'

'Yes, let's!'

'Everyone gather round!'

'One, two, three and a . . .'

The Brownies stood round their pool and when Harry said 'Go!' they all jumped in together with a tremendous splash.

But when they were all in at once there was no room for anybody to try to swim, so Brown Owl told them to get out and take it in turns to swim. Then they jumped in together again, after which she let all the Brownies go in who couldn't swim yet. They tried hard, with one toe on the bottom. At last it was time to come out, but Brown Owl said that they could come again. She would help the new ones to learn to swim every day that the sun shone that week.

The sun went on shining for over a fortnight, and soon all the Brownies could swim except Sassy. Sassy was not really trying very hard. She thought it was more fun to take a long run and jump right into the middle of the pool, and then scramble out and do it all over again.

'Come on, Sassy,' Brown Owl said. 'You don't stay in the pool long enough to try properly. Try all by yourself now. That's right – kick your legs out behind you.'

Sassy tried, but swimming was not fast enough for her. She could move about faster if she ran, so she only stayed in for about half a minute and then jumped out again.

'I'll put my hand under your chin,' Amanda

offered, and this way Amanda was able to hang on to Sassy's bathing-suit so that she could not run away. Very soon Sassy could swim.

But next day she seemed to have forgotten all she had learnt about swimming. Brown Owl had to start again, and Amanda had to hold her up by her chin and the back of her swim-suit. And this time it took much longer before she actually swam two strokes by herself.

'Come on, Sassy!' Amanda said. 'Yesterday you swam five strokes by yourself. You swam right across the pool.' She seized hold of Sassy's cap as her head went under water again. The cap came off in her hand and Sassy's head bobbed up – but it was not Sassy's head. It was Sam's! Everyone had been taken in by his looking exactly like Sassy when his short hair was covered up by her cap.

'Sam's changed places with Sassy!' exclaimed the Brownies.

'He's wearing her bathing-suit!'

'And he was wearing her bathing-cap!'

'Where's Sassy?' Brown Owl wanted to know.

'At home,' said Sam.

'Does she know you've got her things?' Lucinda asked.

'She gave them to me. I wanted to learn to swim.'

'The Brownies were going to teach brothers and sisters on the French Day,' Brown Owl said. 'I'm afraid you'll have to wait till then.'

'That's no good,' said Sam. 'I want to learn before I go to France.'

'Only Brownies are going to France,' Lucinda told him.

'I'm not going with the Brownies,' said Sam. 'I'm going by myself.'

Brown Owl laughed and Sam got dry, put on his clothes and went home.

Presently Sassy came running up the hill.

'Sam says you saw it was him!' she panted. 'Is there time for me, too? Can I have my bathe, too?' She was taking off her clothes as she ran.

'But your swim-suit's all wet,' Brown Owl said. 'You'll catch cold.'

'No, I won't, and I'll be wet anyway. Please let me, Brown Owl, because I want to swim across the pool again.' And before Brown Owl had time to say any more, Sassy had struggled into her wet bathing-suit, jumped into the water and was puffing her way across.

Lucinda helped her to dry afterwards.

'Does Sam really think he's going to France?' Lucinda asked Sassy.

'He says he is.'

'Well, he can't come with us,' declared Lucinda.

'He doesn't want to.'

'And I don't see how a little boy can go by himself.'

'Oh, Sam can, if he really wants to,' said Sassy.

'Anyway, he won't have enough money,' said Lucinda.

'He says he's going to do up the bicycle and sell it.'

'It's only worth a few pence,' said Lucinda.

'Sam's going to get two pounds for it,' said Sassy.

'Nobody'll want to buy it.'

'He's going to have a Jumble Sale all of his own,' said Sassy, and she squeezed her bathing-suit and wrapped it up in her towel. 'And Sam says you'll be very sorry if the Brownies don't let him learn to swim in this pool,' she ended up.

'Sam's a very silly little boy,' said Brown Owl. 'And it's time you went home.'

Next day when the Brownies came to bathe in their pool they found that there was no water in it. Somebody had dug and dug into the bank so that the stream had gone back into its old course, and the haystack cover lay empty except for a few bits of grass and a newt. The Brownies were so astonished when they saw it that Tawny, coming up the path, could hear the noise they made hundreds of yards away. It was a sort of an 'он!', and a groan all at once. And then everybody looked at Sassy.

'How could Sam do it alone?' Lucinda said.

'He didn't,' a voice said.

'Oh, Sassy!' said Brown Owl. 'You didn't help him, did you?'

'A Brownie helps other people every day, especially those at home,' said Sassy. 'We weren't at home, but Sam belongs to home.'

'And you spoilt our beautiful new pool just because Sam got cross.'

'It was very difficult,' said Sassy. 'We were very, very surprised when the water ran the other way again.'

'Sassy, I'm afraid I shall have to talk to you after Brownies,' said Brown Owl with a deep sigh.

It was no good anybody thinking there was going to be any swimming that afternoon. It would take Harry and all the Brownies half a day to make the water go back again to run through the pool, and Harry was not here today. So the Brownies picked up their bathing things sadly and went home, leaving Brown Owl and Sassy by themselves.

'Sassy, I'm very sorry to have to tell you,' said Brown Owl, 'that unless you try much harder to be helpful, we shan't be able to take you to France.'

'Me not go to France?' exclaimed Sassy.

'Not if you go on doing such silly things,' said Brown Owl. 'I know Sam makes you, but when he has a bad idea like spoiling the pool, you must try to stop him doing it, instead of doing it, too.'

Sassy hung her head. 'Yes, it was a bad idea,' she said softly. 'Very bad. Now we can't swim in it.'

'Of course you can't swim in it. Didn't you know that when you were digging?'

'Yes, but Sam thought it would be a good joke,' said Sassy.

'Try hard to keep your Brownie Promise,' Brown Owl said, 'and then I promise you shall come to France.'

Next day Brown Owl said the Brownies could practise swimming in the river.

There was a good place with a kind of natural swimming-pool. It has grassy banks on three sides and a shallow end for shaky swimmers, and a deeper end, near the river proper, for surer swimmers. Here the Brownies practised nearly every day, and Harry taught some of them to dive off the bank.

'All curl your toes over the edge of the bank,' he said. 'Point your fingers above your heads to start with, and then swing out as you leap so that you dive into the water in a straight line, like a row of pencils. Turn your fingers up when you want to come to the surface. Ready, steady, dive!'

Five Brownies dived, and Amanda even managed to open her eyes under the water and see, in a blurred and brownish kind of way, what was going on. All five Brownies came up together.

'You looked more like a row of pin cushions than pencils,' Harry said. 'But never mind, it was a good start.'

'I want to try,' Sassy said.

'You've only just learned to swim,' Harry objected.

'But I *can* swim,' she said, and before Harry could stop her she had dived off the bank looking, at any rate, more like a pencil than a pin cushion.

So next time there were six Brownies in Harry's diving row.

That was what decided Brown Owl to enter the Pack for the Divisional Swimming Gala. She explained that it was a great day of swimming sports when most of the Packs in the Division met.

'Would we win prizes?' Lucinda asked at once.

'If you win a race or diving or life-saving competition, then you score points for the Pack. These are added up and the Pack with the most points wins a shield and keeps it for a year.'

'We must win the shield,' the Brownies shouted.

The Gala was held in a big covered swimming pool. All the Brownies who were swimming in it (including Sassy, who was in a diving competition) changed into swim-suits, and the others went up into the gallery to watch.

The Gala began with the life-saving competition and to Amanda's amazement she won the most points for her Pack. From then onwards sometimes their Pack won and sometimes another one did, but when it came to the last event theirs was very near the top.

The final event was the Relay race. Amanda, as the fastest swimmer in the Pack, was to swim last. She saw Tulip swimming towards her in line with the others and got ready to dive in but suddenly a twist of cramp ran down her side.

'What's the matter?' Jeanie asked behind her.

'Cramp,' said Amanda, bending double. 'I can't swim.' She knew she had spoilt the race for the Pack. She knew they could not possibly win the shield now, but it was no use trying to jump in the water. She could not even move.

Tulip got nearer and nearer, with the other Brownies swimming just behind her. She touched the end and there was no one from their Pack to go on with the race.

Then suddenly, almost over the top of Amanda, somebody dived in. Amanda stared and saw Sassy, swimming hard towards the far end. The other Brownies swam hard too, but Sassy was ahead of them. Amanda's cramp disappeared as she saw

Sassy touch the side before the others – and win. And that meant they had won the shield!

'Oh dear,' said Brown Owl, 'perhaps changing the team in the middle isn't allowed,' and she went to find out.

She came back beaming. 'It's all right,' she said. 'Each team is allowed a spare, and although we hadn't made Sassy our spare, she was wonderfully quick at coming in at the right second.'

'Wasn't it helpful of her?' Amanda said, looking proudly at the newest Brownie in the Pack.

8 · Set-back for Sassy

At last school ended and the holidays began. That left only two more weeks before the day before France.

Sassy was just as good now as any other Brownie, and sometimes even better. She helped her mother from the moment the first baby woke up, all through the day till the last child shut its eyes and went to sleep. She fetched and carried and rocked the cradle and gave the baby its bottles and brought in the washing. She went shopping for her mother, and even sometimes stopped Sam from being quite so terrible.

'Am I all right for France?' she asked Brown Owl, at the last Brownies but one before they were going.

'Oh, yes, Sassy,' Brown Owl said. 'Of course you'll be able to come.'

'That's good, because you promised.'

And then something terrible happened. Amanda

went home with Sassy, and there sitting round the table were all the little brothers and sisters and babies, and nearly all of them were covered with spots.

'They've got the measles,' said their mother. 'If you haven't had it, Amanda, you'd better not come in.'

'Yes, I've had measles,' said Amanda, 'but what about Sassy?'

'The twins haven't had it yet, but I expect they will. If they don't get it today, they'll get it two weeks today. My children always come out with measles exactly two weeks apart. They always have done, and I expect they always will.'

'Two weeks today!' Amanda said thoughtfully. 'Oh, dear, that's the day we go to France! Then Sassy won't be going if she doesn't get it today.'

For the first time since Sassy had become a Brownie, Amanda saw her cry. Poor Sassy! How she cried!

'But Brown Owl promised!' she sobbed. 'I promised, and she promised.'

'Brown Owl didn't know that you might have measles, though,' Amanda tried to comfort her.

'Perhaps you've got the measles today,' said her mother hopefully. 'Then you'll get over it in time. Do you feel ill?'

'Not a bit,' wailed Sassy. 'I feel very well, and I

want to go to France. I must go to France. Brown Owl said I'm all right to go to France.'

Sam came in and his mother looked him up and down. He sat down with the others. Amanda looked, too, to see if she could see any signs of any spots, but there were none. The children on either side of him were like pink plum-puddings, their faces were so spotty.

'Perhaps you won't get measles, Sassy,' said Amanda. 'Then you can come to France.'

'Oh, no, she can't,' said her mother, 'because if she doesn't get it two weeks today, she'll get it from one of the other children later on, and she'll be infectious.'

'Supposing she didn't see any of the other children after today,' Amanda asked, 'then would she be all right?'

'She still might get it a fortnight today,' persisted her mother.

'Don't worry, Sassy,' said Amanda. 'I think I've had an idea. I'm going home now, but I'll come back later.'

Amanda ran home across the fields, thinking to herself. 'Oh, dear, what bad luck it would be, if after Sassy had tried so hard to be good and helpful, she has to stay at home on the day abroad.'

Meanwhile Sassy cried so hard that she could eat no tea, and her mother was quite sure that she must already have measles. Her face was almost as red as her spotty brothers and sisters.

'If you've got measles now,' said her mother, 'there's nothing to worry about. You'll be quite all right in time for the outing.'

Sassy stopped crying with almost a crash. She looked up with her eyes wide open with relief.

'You mean if I've got measles today, I can go?' she asked again.

'Yes,' said her mother, 'with any luck.'

Sam heard what she said, too, and without finishing his bread and dripping he jumped up and whisked Sassy out of the room. When she came back she was limping slightly and Sam had to help her along.

'Yes, I do feel ill after all,' she said.

'She's really bad,' said Sam. 'You've only got to look at her.'

Their mother looked at her and saw that her face was just as covered in spots as any of the others.

'Except that you haven't got any spots on your

hands or your knees,' their mother said, and she pulled Sassy towards her. With a flannel she washed half the spots off with one long wipe. 'Oh, you are a silly couple! Did you really think I couldn't tell a bit of paint from the real thing?'

Sassy was very sorry that her mother had not been taken in, but now she felt a little bit hungry, so with one side of her face still spotty she sat down to eat some tea. She was sitting there with the others when Amanda came back, and with Amanda was her mother.

'I'm so sorry to hear about the measles,' said Amanda's mother.

'Oh, well,' said the twins' mother, 'they've got to get it some time, and it's nice weather for it.'

'If Sassy gets it before they go to France, of course she won't be able to go,' Amanda's mother said. 'But supposing she doesn't, she'll just have time to be out of quarantine.'

'She would have time if she wasn't all the time with children who've already got measles.'

'Exactly,' said Amanda's mother. 'That's just what I mean. I was thinking that if Sassy came to stay with Amanda, she wouldn't see the other children. Of course she may get measles, but if she doesn't, she'll be all right.'

'Me go and stay at your farm?' Sassy said when she understood. 'That would be almost as good as France!'

'We could have great fun as it's holidays,' Amanda said. 'You could help to feed the calves and bring in the eggs.'

'Well, if you're sure you don't mind,' the twins' mother said, 'of course she can. But what if she gets measles?'

'We'll look after her,' said Amanda's mother. 'You see, I've only got one and I have plenty of time.'

'There's one other thing,' said Amanda. 'Sam!'

'I was thinking of Sam,' said the twins' mother. 'Sam mustn't follow Sassy or go near her. If he does, and he's got measles and she hasn't, it'll spoil the whole thing.'

'I'll tell Sam he mustn't come,' said Sassy.

'If she tells him, he won't,' said her mother. 'Those two are as thick as thieves.'

'I want to go to France, Sam,' said Sassy. 'Only you're not to stop me by giving me your old measles.'

'I want to go to France, too,' said Sam. 'That's why I'm not going to get measles.'

'Is he really going to France?' Amanda's mother asked the twins' mother.

'It's the first I've heard of it,' said the twins' mother. 'Unless the Brownies are taking him.'

'No. We're having a French Day when we get back for him and all the other brothers and sisters,'

Amanda said, 'but we can't take any of them with us when we really go to France.'

'Then shall we take Sassy back with us now?' Amanda's mother asked.

'She's not ready to go away.' The twins' mother began to fluster round. 'She's hardly got any clean clothes, and I haven't washed her hair.'

'That doesn't matter,' said Amanda. 'She can wash her hair at the farm.'

'And she doesn't need much on the farm,' said Amanda's mother.

'All I want is my Brownie's uniform and what I've got on,' said Sassy.

'You'll need more than that,' said her mother. 'I'll go and see what I can find,' and she went upstairs, leaving Amanda and her mother to keep an eye on all the children. The measly ones were not very hungry, and were beginning to look miserable and wanting to go to bed.

The twins' mother came down the stairs with a little bag full of Sassy's clothes.

'I don't know how I shall manage without Sassy,' she said cheerfully. 'She's been such a help lately. Still, the change will do her good. But who knows, maybe she won't get measles after all, and then she'll have a nice blow with the others in the Channel.'

Amanda and Sassy and Amanda's mother said goodbye and set off for the farm. Sam saw them go from the cherry tree, and he threw a few half-hearted sticks after them, but did not try to follow.

Sassy had a wonderful time with Amanda at the farm. There were so many lovely things to do, and there was no time to be anything but helpful and nice. There was Amanda's pony, Jason, to ride and to feed and to make a fuss of, and there was her dog, Bob, and all the cows and chickens and turkeys and calves and farm-people to talk to. Sometimes Amanda and Sassy would see Sam's face peering sadly down at them from a tree, but they said nothing and pretended they had not seen it. One thing about his face was that it was not covered in spots yet. Nor was Sassy's, but then their mother had said that in their family measles took exactly two weeks to come out.

Sam never came right into the garden or the farm house. Amanda felt sorrier and sorrier for him having his twin taken away from him, and Sassy got nicer and nicer. When she was not being naughty she was great fun, always laughing and making funny jokes. Amanda never made jokes when she was on her own at the farm, but with somebody to laugh with she made quite a lot. Amanda was very careful not to talk about the French Day in case Sassy couldn't go, and they kept away from the other Brownies just in case Sassy could give them measles.

Sassy was so happy at the farm that she seemed

to have forgotten all about France. Amanda kept looking at Sassy, and so did her mother, but Sassy had no spots and seemed to be feeling quite well.

On the getting-ready day, Sassy had to stay at the farm, because if she was going to have measles she would give it to the others. Today was the last day she might get it. If she was all right when she woke up, then she could go to France. So Sassy stayed with Amanda's mother while Amanda went to Brownies, armed with lots of farm eggs which her mother had hard-boiled for the whole Pack. Tulip had brought plums, Jeanie had brought apples, and Olivia had brought pasties that her mother had made with her help.

'The ones with "O"s on them have got onions inside and the ones that haven't are plain,' she explained. Jean had brought bacon sandwiches, Lucinda had brought chocolate, and Trixie's mother had sent enough seasick pills for the whole Pack, as her mother had said, 'to go almost round the world in comfort'. While they were laying all the things out on the table and deciding how they would divide them up into Sixes, there was a knock at the door.

'Come in!' everybody called at once

In came Pat and Cherry and Mary.

'We've brought something for the day in France,' said Cherry.

'We all wish we were coming, too,' said Pat.

'We shall be thinking of you,' said Mary, and they put on the table a great big bag of barley sugar and a small bag of jelly babies.

'The barley sugar is for when you're on the boat,' said Cherry. 'It's very good for travelling. And the jelly babies are to give to the French children you meet when you get there.'

'How sweet of you to think of us,' said Brown Owl. 'You're off to camp yourselves tomorrow, aren't you?'

'Yes,' said Cherry, 'we shall be leaving at about the same time as you. And we shall still be travelling when you get home in the evening.'

'We're all terribly excited,' said Mary.

'So are we!' called all the Brownies.

'We're going to France and we're going to talk French!'

'And we're going to use French money!'

'And we're going to bring back lots of French food!'

'And we're going to eat lots there!' said Trixie.

'We'll eat a little there,' said Brown Owl. 'We'll

have French bread and *pâté* and French fruit for
our lunch, shall we? And the rest of the things we
buy we'll bring home for our French Day. We don't
want to eat so much food that we are ill on the way
back.'

'All this,' Tulip pointed out, 'is for our breakfast
on the train and for our "elevenses" on the boat.'

'What are we going to drink?' asked Lucinda.

'Milk for breakfast,' Amanda said, 'because it
won't travel well for longer than that. I'm bringing
some from the farm.'

'And orangeade for "elevenses",' said Ann.

'And French drinks for lunch,' said Olivia.

'What about tea?'

'More French drinks,' said Lucinda. 'French
people don't have tea like we do.'

'And tea on the boat with supper coming back,'
suggested Brown Owl.

The Guides went away and each Six packed up
its food. Brown Owl and Tawny went round to
look at the way they had done it and to see their
first-aid-kits, which had bandages and gauze and
sticking-plaster and sunburn cream and insect re-
pellent in case they were troubled by midges. The
Kelpies also had a very good supply of clean
handkerchiefs, and Brown Owl suggested that the
others Sixes should bring some, too, next day.

'We'll meet at the station,' said Brown Owl, 'at
seven o'clock. Everybody must wear Brownie uni-

form with a jersey on, and everybody must bring a mac.'

'But we'll be much too hot,' said Lucinda. 'If it's a lovely day like today, we shan't need either.'

'Even if it's a lovely day,' said Brown Owl, 'it'll be very cold in the morning, and you've no idea how blowy it is on the boat. And everyone will need bathing things and bathing towels.'

'I shall bring a thick one,' said Tulip, 'to wrap round me if it's cold coming home.'

'You must all go to bed very early tonight,' said Brown Owl. 'But before you go to bed lay out all your clothes and all the things you'll need, so you won't be a bother to your mothers in the morning.'

'I'm going to bed so early,' said Trixie, 'that I'm going straight home to bed now!'

'Aren't you going to have any tea?' asked Jeanie.

'Yes, I'll have a big tea and then go straight to sleep.'

The Brownies all romped off home, and Amanda's last words to Brown Owl were:

'I do hope Sassy won't have any spots when I get back. She wants to come so terribly.'

9 · The journey begins

Sassy was all right and all ready to go next day. Amanda helped her to lay out her uniform and jersey and macintosh, and they both went to bed very early, just as Brown Owl had said they should.

Sassy was the first to wake next morning, and she crept into Amanda's room and shook her arm. 'Wake up, Amanda, we mustn't miss the boat!' she said.

They dressed very quietly, and went down to the kitchen. Amanda put the kettle on while Sassy got a tea-tray ready for tea for Amanda's mother and father, so she could take it up to them as a surprise.

Amanda carried it up and her mother was very pleased with the tea, but her father was still sound asleep.

'I'm coming with you to the station,' her mother said. 'You'd better have some tea yourselves before we start.'

'We have,' said Sassy. 'We've poured out two mugs full in the kitchen.'

They all set off for the station, where several Brownies and their mothers were waiting on the platform. Brown Owl was there, too, and Tawny, and Harry had come to see them off. Everybody was there long before the train came in, and seasick pills were handed round. When it came they all packed in and shouted and waved good-bye to their mothers, as though they were going away for a long Pack Holiday instead of just for the day.

When the train started, each Sixer unpacked her breakfast bag and passed the food round to her Six, after she had given some to Brown Owl and Tawny.

It was a grey, hazy morning that looked very hopeful for later on. All the Brownies were glad it was not too bright, for they knew that might mean rain to follow. The cows were grazing contentedly in the fields as the train rushed past them. Sometimes they passed a dog, but there were very few people about yet.

Almost as soon as they had finished breakfast, Brown Owl warned them to gather up their things as they were going to change trains at the next station. Out they all poured when the train stopped, and then they had to wait for another one. It was not a very long wait, but just long enough for the Pack to stretch their legs by hopping and jumping about. The next train was a longer one, and there were already some people in it on their way to work. One man asked the Kelpies where they were going.

'We're going to France,' said Sassy, proudly.

The man looked very surprised.

'Oh, well,' he said, 'the weather forecast's good. You should have a lovely time.'

At Newhaven the train seemed to run right on to the Quay. They could see the masts of the boats beside them, and when they got out and crossed a foot-bridge on to another platform, there was their boat all ready waiting for them.

'It's not very big.' said Tulip.

'Big enough for us,' said Tawny.

Brown Owl had to show all their papers and tickets, and then they were allowed to go across the gangway on to the boat. Once they were aboard it

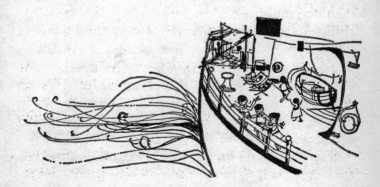

seemed much bigger, and Amanda was sure they would get lost.

'You'd better hold my hand, Sassy,' she told her, 'and don't go near the rails.'

There were already a lot of people on board who had arrived by earlier trains or by car, and had settled themselves on all the seats on deck.

'We'd better go below,' said Brown Owl, 'to find somewhere where we can put all our things and sit when we get tired.'

So they went down a broad staircase and along a passage with doors each side. Notices said that the doors on one side led to cabins and, on the other, to offices.

'Are we going to have cabins?' asked Trixie. 'Will we go to sleep in them?' She had caught sight of a bunk in one small cabin whose door was open.

'We don't need to go to sleep,' said Olivia, 'it won't be night-time.'

Then they came to rows of seats and most of these were filled up, too. Sassy let go of Amanda's hand and ran on ahead into the refreshment-room, where passengers were sitting at tables drinking coffee or buying sandwiches at a counter in the middle. Sassy turned off into a little compartment of slatted shelves.

'Here's a cabin for us!' she cried, climbing up on to the top shelf.

'That's meant for luggage,' Brown Owl explained.

'All the same,' said Tawny, 'it's not a bad place to be. As it's a day trip there won't be any luggage, and we could stuff all the Brownies and all the bags on the shelves when they're not running about.'

'I'll ask a steward,' said Brown Owl, and she went and asked a man in uniform. He thought it would be a very good idea to make the luggage compartment a kind of camp for the Brownies.

They all rushed in and climbed up on to the shelves, and then peered through the slats at all the people passing by. There was even a porthole, so they could look out at the sea.

'We can pretend we're animals in a cage,' suggested Tulip, growling through the slats.

When the Brownies had sorted themselves out, Brown Owl and Tawny took them exploring all over the boat, and they just happened to be on the deck as the gangway was pulled away and the boat cast off. Very slowly she moved away from the quay and the Brownies waved and shouted: 'Goodbye, England!' and a sailor on the quay grinned and waved back.

There were a lot of boys watching the sea-gulls on the other side of the deck, and they had two or three men in charge of them.

'That's a choir outing,' said Lucinda. 'I heard them saying so to the ticket man.'

It was very smooth in the harbour, but as soon as they got out into the open sea the boat began to rock. They looked back at the hilly cliffs. They seemed to have been cut out of the Downs as though someone had baked a great big cake rather unevenly, and then cut it across the middle. The sun was shining steadily now, and the water sparkled. A good stiff breeze blew the Brownies' hair across their faces. The cliffs began to grow smaller.

Brown Owl decided that it was time for 'elevenses', so the Pack went down to their 'cage' to eat apples and barley sugar and drink orangeade. Brown Owl and Tawny had some coffee from the refreshment bar, which Amanda and Tulip fetched them as a surprise. When they had finished, the two Sixers took back the empty cups and saucers. On the other side of the counter the choirboys were all drinking ginger beer out of bottles through straws.

Suddenly Tulip stiffened and then jogged Amanda's arm.

'Look,' she said urgently, 'but don't look as though you're looking.'

'What is it?' Amanda asked.

'Don't let him see you. Look! In a red jersey! Just behind the tallest choir boy.' She was talking out of the side of her mouth.

Amanda looked and there, to her amazement, was Sam, also drinking ginger beer through a straw out of a bottle.

'But Sam's not a choirboy,' Amanda whispered.

'Anyway they're not our choirboys,' Tulip whispered back. 'Shall we tell Brown Owl?'

'Perhaps they've asked him to go with them. Then we'd look silly,' said Amanda. 'I'm sure Sassy doesn't know.'

'We'd better not tell Sassy, or she might dash off with him,' said Tulip.

They went back to the Pack, and several times when they were walking about the boat with Brown Owl and Tawny, they caught sight of Sam. He was careful to keep the choirboys between him and the Brownie Pack.

Now when they went on deck they could see nothing but sea all around them. The cliffs had faded into the distance. The choir outing was sitting on deck near a life boat and the choirmaster was handing out sausage rolls.

Suddenly Amanda heard him say: 'Somebody's had two! There were just enough for one each and there isn't one for Peter!'

Amanda could just see Sam tucked away almost under the life-boat, munching away at a sausage roll. The choirmaster started to count the boys. 'Fifteen,' he counted. 'There's something wrong here. There should only be fourteen.' And suddenly he saw Sam. 'Hey, you – you're not one of the choir. What are you doing here?'

The small boy next to him turned pink. 'I'm

sorry, sir. I thought he was the new boy you said was joining the choir soon. He's been with us all the time.'

'I am the new choirboy,' Sam said stoutly.

'You're certainly not!' said the choirmaster. 'He had red hair and freckles, and anyway, you have to sing in the choir for a year before you can come on an outing like this. Go on! Be off with you!'

But Sam stayed where he was.

'Who's looking after you?' asked the choir-master.

'Nobody,' said Sam. 'I'm looking after myself.'

'Who brought you aboard, then?'

'You did!' said Sam. 'I came with your lot.'

'Well, I didn't buy you a ticket,' said the choir-master.

'That's all right,' said Sam, 'I know you didn't.'

'I think I'd better take you to the purser,' said the choirmaster, but Sam shrank back under the life-boat.

'Look out!' said one of the boys quickly. 'You'll fall into the sea!' and he dragged him back to safety.

'I don't want to go to the purser!' Sam started to kick, and at that moment Sassy saw him.

Instantly she dashed away from the Brownies, shouting angrily at the choirboys. 'Put my brother down! Leave him alone! How dare you!'

The boys let go and Sam disappeared between

the others. Brown Owl followed Sassy in amazement.

'I'm so sorry,' the choirmaster said with a smile to Brown Owl. 'I didn't realize he was yours. He got mixed up with ours and started eating some of their lunch.'

'He's not exactly ours,' said Brown Owl, 'and I don't know how he got here.'

'He *is* ours!' Sassy said. 'He's my brother! He said he was coming to France.'

'I can't think how he got to Newhaven,' Brown Owl said. 'In fact, I can't think how he got here at all. I'm sure he hasn't got a ticket.'

'I expect he's a stowaway,' said Sassy proudly. 'He said he would be.'

'I'm terribly sorry he ate some of your food. We'll give you some of ours.'

'Don't worry,' said the choirmaster. 'We've got plenty, really. It just seemed so odd that there wasn't enough to go round. Will you look after him now?'

'If we can find him,' said Brown Owl ruefully. 'Come on, Brownies, we'll all look for Sam together.'

So they went round the boat, asking people if they had seen a little boy with brown shorts and a red jersey. But nobody had. Amanda held tightly on to Sassy's hand.

'Did you know he was coming?'

'He said he was, didn't he?' Sassy said.

'It was very naughty of him,' said Amanda.

'Rather naughty of him,' Sassy said.

But Sam was nowhere to be seen, and Brown Owl took the Brownies back to their 'cage' and they stayed with Tawny playing guessing games, while Brown Owl went off to have another look by herself.

'It's no good,' she said, when she came back, 'there's not a sign of him. He must be hiding somewhere. Perhaps we shall see him when he comes off the boat. He'll have to come along with us now he's got so far.'

'We've got plenty of food,' Tulip said. 'We can easily share it with him.'

'What a worry for his mother,' Brown Owl said.

'She won't worry,' said Sassy. 'He often goes out

all day, and when he's hungry he eats blackberries.'

Now the Brownies all went up on deck for Brown Owl to show them a thin, faint shadow on the water. 'That's France,' she said.

A cheer broke out among the Brownies.

'It's not a bit how I thought,' said Trixie. 'It's a much cloudier place.'

'It's only because it's so far away,' Amanda explained.

Gradually the land looked firmer, and the Brownies could see trees and the roofs of houses. Soon it was time to go down and collect up all their baggage and queue up on deck with all the other passengers, ready for when the boat docked. They glided past the lighthouse and into the harbour, and there the Brownies saw all sorts of little boats and dredgers and fishermen, and French children running along the quay with their mothers.

'It's like a silent film,' said Amanda. 'It doesn't seem real.'

The boat slid along between great posts, and beyond it the Brownies could see the town of Dieppe, brightly coloured, with lots of gay notices that they could not understand. They could see shops and cafés, and people hurrying about and a train that seemed to be going along the road. The boat stopped, and soon the gangway was pulled up and people began to stream off the boat. All the Brownies watched carefully for Sam. But there was no sign of him. Soon it was their turn to cross the gangway, and when they were all on the quay and there were no more people to come off, Brown Owl went up to the man at the bottom of the gangway to tell him that Sam was lost.

But the man was not at all worried and told her that he would probably turn up, and if he was still in the boat they were not to worry.

But Brown Owl looked very worried. 'I know we

'didn't bring him,' she said, 'but he is Sassy's twin, and he belongs to our village.'

'Let's go to the sands,' said Tawny, 'and have lunch, and then we'll come back and ask again.'

So the Brownies all followed Brown Owl to the sandy shore that was a little way away from the harbour. They looked about them as they went, and they listened to the children chatting away with their mothers in French. They decided that the French they had learnt at Brownies was not going to be much use for making friends in. On the way to the sands they passed very bright-looking shops, where Brown Owl had said they could buy their French lunch. But none of the Brownies felt nearly French enough yet to try. In fact, Trixie was rather nervous, especially when she passed a French policeman with a gun.

'Do you think he knows we're not French?' she asked the others anxiously, as though they were doing something wrong by not being French. So in the end Brown Owl and Tawny, who knew lots of French, had to buy the food and the Brownies listened amazed. They came away from the shops with armfuls of long, thin sticks of bread and some French butter and some potted meat that Brown Owl had told them was specially good. At the fruit shop they bought an enormous bag full of yellowy-red plums that Brown Owl called 'mirabelles'.

Then they went down to the shore and walked

across the finest sand any of them had ever seen. It was so soft and lovely that they took off their shoes and socks at once, so that they could feel their toes curling into it, as they walked. There was a row of brightly-coloured bathing-huts and then, beyond them, more sand, and this is where they sat down to eat their first French meal.

Afterwards they exchanged their uniforms for bathing-suits. The food had been lovely, and the plums delicious, and the sun made them feel all sleepy and happy. Amanda was lying in a little dip in the sand when she noticed a brown hand stretch out and take a handful of plums from the little pile in front of her. Sleepily she looked up and saw that in some mysterious way Sam was sharing the picnic.

Brown Owl saw him at the same time, and jumped to her feet. 'How did you get off the boat, Sam?' she asked.

'Walked,' said Sam, and he would say no more.

'Well, now you're here, you will have to stay with us,' said Brown Owl.

'And share our food,' said the Brownies willingly, 'and swim with us, and play games with us.'

Sam peeled off his shirt, and settled down in the sand beside the others. Brown Owl sighed. She had said that no little brothers or sisters were to come, and Sam had come, and there was nothing more she could do about it except look after him with the others.

Some of the Brownies drifted off into a sunny doze, but presently everybody began to wake up. Children in sun-suits appeared from the tents and huts and started to play games. Brown Owl and Tawny were in swim-suits by this time and they started up a game of Twos and Threes with the Brownies. Sam joined in. A small brown French boy joined in, too, and gradually more and more French children crept or ran full tilt into the game. Nobody cared that the Brownies could not speak French, though one or two of the French children could speak a few words of English. Soon the Brownies were calling out French words they heard the other children using, for it was quite clear that '*deux*' meant 'two' and '*trois*' meant 'three', that '*ici*' meant 'here' and '*là*' meant 'there'. It was a wonderful game.

When an hour had passed since their last meal, Brown Owl said the Brownies could bathe, and several of the French children bathed with them and, of course, Sam. Brown Owl went into the water with the Brownies, and Tawny stood on the edge all ready to rush to anybody's help if they needed it. Harry's pool at home had been such a help that all the Brownies could swim now, and nobody needed Tawny. They all came out to dry in the sun, and they hardly needed their towels at all.

'Shall we go shopping next, Brown Owl, and use our French francs?' Lucinda asked. Then they handed round the jelly babies to the French children.

Everybody thought this was a very good idea. A little French girl, who understood that they had just come for the day, showed them where they could leave all their bathing things and bags in her tent while they went shopping. Tulip tried to sign to her that perhaps she might like to come, too, and show them the way. She signed back that she would have to stay on the sands because her old grandmother (she pointed to her in a deck-chair) liked her to be there to run messages for her. It was wonderful to find that they could really understand each other with only a few words of each other's languages.

The Brownies set off for the town and wandered down the main street looking at the shops, gazing at the marvellous fruit stalls and the long-whiskered prawns and mussels in their shells on the fish stalls. There was so much to see, and so much that they would like to buy. But they decided not to buy anything till they had been all the way to the top of the street, and then they would do their shopping on the way back. They paused at the top to watch some French people playing tennis and other French people diving into a huge swimming-pool. There were flowers everywhere in tubs and flower-beds, and round the entrance to the ancient castle.

They turned round and started back. Now began the real marketing, and all the Brownies felt so at home in France that everyone of them asked for something in French. Everybody said '*S'il vous plaît*' for 'please' till the bags were full of pastries and chocolate coins, and marzipan animals, and fruit, and prawns and mussels – rather smelly – and picture postcards and sweets made like pebbles, and little glass windmills and cheese, and long French loaves. By the time they had reached the bottom of the street, where most of the cafés had tables outside overlooking the harbour, they were all quite tired, but very happy. Brown Owl bought them all ice cream cones that had three compartments –

one for lemon ice-cream, one for raspberry and one for chocolate. None of them had ever tasted anything so good. Suddenly, Brown Owl realised that she had two ice-creams over. She looked quickly round, counting heads. Two children were missing.

'Sassy and Sam!' cried several Brownies all at once.

'When did you last see them?' Brown Owl asked.

'By the swimming-pool.'

'By the tennis-court.'

'By the castle.'

'Yes, by the castle.'

'We haven't seen them since we were by the castle.'

'Had they any money?' Brown Owl asked.

'Yes, Sassy had some.'

Brown Owl sighed. 'So I suppose they spent it on getting inside and going up to see the ruins. I'd better go back.'

'I'll come with you,' offered Amanda.

'All right. And you'd better all go back to the shore with Tawny.'

'We haven't got any shells yet, or seaweed, or sea-sponges,' said the Brownies, and so they all went to the sands, while Brown Owl and Amanda started back up the street looking on both sides for the twins as they went. Of course Amanda saw all sorts of things in the shops that she had missed before, but there was no time to stop now. They reached the gate in the castle wall, and Brown Owl asked if the twins had been seen, but nobody had noticed them. She bought tickets and they went in. Although they went everywhere they were allowed to, there was no sign of the twins.

'Perhaps they've gone back to the others,' said Amanda.

The town hall clock clanked out the hour.

'It's nearly time we went back to the boat. I expect the others'll be on their way there already,' said Brown Owl.

Amanda thought of the boat and the Brownies going aboard, and all the other people going aboard, and of the gang-plank being removed, and of the boat slowly moving out to return to England without the twins.

'Perhaps the twins'll go straight back to the boat,' Brown Owl said. 'They will notice all the English people going that way.'

The street forked, and in the fork there were café tables that seemed to be almost part of the street.

'Let's sit here for a minute and have a cool down,' said Amanda, who suddenly felt she could not go on. The climb to the castle in the sun had made her feel quite dizzy.

'All right,' said Brown Owl. 'Then we can watch all three streets at once.' She looked at the time. 'We've still got half an hour before the boat leaves.'

The waiter brought them iced lemonade that

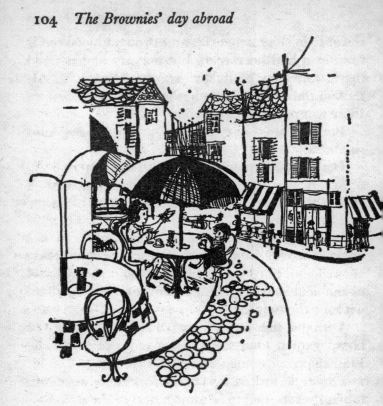

was bright yellow and tasted curiously enough, of orangepeel. Amanda had hardly begun to drink hers when she saw Sassy dawdling along on the other side of the street all by herself.

'There's Sassy!' she shouted, pointing, and Brown Owl jumping up, ran across to her and led her back.

Sassy's face was red from crying, and her beret was pushed on to the back of her head. 'I thought I was lost, and you'd all gone home to England without me, and left me behind,' she wailed.

'Of course we wouldn't do that,' Brown Owl assured her. 'Here, take my lemonade and tell me where Sam is.'

'He suddenly wasn't there, and I stopped to look for him.'

'Did he go into the castle?'

'I don't know.'

'Did you go in?'

'No. I just looked for Sam. I looked everywhere.'

'Perhaps he's gone to the sands, and then to the boat with the others.' Brown Owl paid for the drinks, and they all got up and made their way through the still-crowded street towards the quay. There were so many people, they had to walk half on the pavement and half on the road to get along fast enough, and every now and then Sassy, who had suddenly cheered up like anything with the lemonade, stopped to look in a shop window, and they thought they had lost her again.

What a relief it was at any rate to see the Pack all crowded round the gangway waiting to go aboard when they came. There was only one thing wrong – there was no Sam.

They waited a bit longer while Tawny handed round a few seasick pills, and Brown Owl went back to the end of the quay. Then she came back to tell the Pack to go aboard, while she went to tell the police about Sam.

11 · Set-back for Sam

On board, Tawny and the Brownies asked everyone they met if they had seen a little boy like Sam. They only had to point out Sassy to show exactly what he looked like, but nobody had seen him. Brown Owl came back to say that the whole boat would have to be held up until Sam was found. Now some of the passengers began to feel rather cross with the Brownies, who they knew were the cause of the delay. Half an hour passed with the gangway down, with nobody but Brown Owl using it as she kept coming back to see if Sam was on board.

'The police are looking for him in the town,' she said.

'I don't mind staying behind,' offered Tulip, 'and then the boat can sail. If I find him, we can sleep somewhere for the night and then come on the next boat tomorrow.'

'It's very sweet of you,' Brown Owl smiled. 'I was thinking of doing the same myself. But supposing he's somewhere on the boat, then we would be staying behind unnecessarily, Tulip. Anyway, apparently the police won't let the boat sail while any of the passengers are left behind.' She went to the end of the quay again, and all the Brownies stood on the deck and watched her go.

And then, suddenly, there was great excitement round the gangway with the police and the officers of the boat. They jabbered so fast in French that none of the Brownies could understand a word of what was being shouted. But they *could* understand that Brown Owl was needed back on the boat again, so Amanda stood at the very end of the deck and sent a message to Brown Owl along the quay in semaphore, which she had luckily been learning for her Highway badge:

'PLEASE COME BACK! YOU ARE WANTED!'

And then out of the confusion of French came the news that Sam was apparently on board after all.

'DO NOT WORRY — SAM SAFELY ABOARD'

they signalled.

They could see that Brown Owl was not worrying, but she did hurry even more than before. Soon the gangway was begin pulled away again with Brown Owl safely on board. There was no sign of

Sam, but the Brownies supposed that the captain had been so annoyed with him over the hold-up that he had kept him in his cabin.

The only people in the Pack who had not hurried towards Brown Owl when she came aboard were Tulip and Sassy. They were still standing watching the cast off and listening to the cries of the sailors in French as the boat began to move. But suddenly a cry even louder than theirs came from Sassy. She pointed to the very end of the quay, where the shops and café were.

'There he is! There's Sam! Look, he's not on board at all!'

Tulip saw his red jersey, too, and started to shout back to Brown Owl that Sam was on the quay.

They all looked and there, sure enough, was Sam, strolling along with his hands in his pockets in no hurry at all. He even stopped to buy a postcard and some sticky sweets from one of the street vendors who had been trying to persuade the passengers to give up the last of their French change before they went aboard.

All the Brownies yelled at him at once. Brown Owl had to tell them to be quiet while she made herself heard telling the captain. Bells clanged and the boat stopped and reversed, and this time one of the officers crossed the gangway when it was pulled out, and the Brownies saw him go up to Sam. He was shaking his fist at him, talking to him very fast in French. Sam must have understood a bit, because he suddenly ducked as though he was about to be hit and rushed ahead of the officer up the gang-plank and on to the deck. Another officer appeared and asked for his ticket, but Sam had no ticket.

Now the boat could leave and the gangway was pulled up again for the last time, and once again the painters were thrown aboard. By now everyone was so cross with Sam and with Sam's party for having anything to do with him, that the officer who asked for the ticket would not hear of allowing Sam to leave his side till it was paid for. Brown Owl only just had enough money left for tea for all the Brownies down in the refreshment room. Sadly she had to give this money up for Sam's ticket.

The Pack trooped down to the luggage 'cage' they had had before. All the Brownies turned out their pockets and between them they found they had just enough money after all for everybody to have tea.

The boat slid slowly away out of the harbour, and the Brownies who were looking out of the porthole were just able to see the last of the town, with its shops and gay cafés and brightly-coloured bathing-tents. Soon they could only see the masts of the sailing-boats tied up in the harbour, and then there was nothing left of France but a bluey-grey blur. The ship's siren gave a great bleating sigh, and the

moment the boat left the harbour she began to rock. Amanda looked out of the porthole and saw that there were not just white horses on the tops of the waves, but that the waves themselves were building up like hills.

'Let's go up and have a look at those lovely waves from the deck,' Amanda suggested.

'Yes, let's,' said Brown Owl. 'The fresh air will do us all good now we've had our tea.'

So the Brownies went up with Brown Owl and Tawny and they stood in the prow of the boat, and every time it hit a big wave there was a great shower of spray. They all squeaked, rushed and stampeded a few steps backwards. The sea was getting rougher and rougher, but none of the Brownies minded, because they had all had their seasick pills. But Sam had not. Soon Sam turned as pale green as new leaves in spring, and was leaning against the back of a deck-chair, looking too ill even to manage to creep on to it.

'Oh, dear, I think Sam's going to be sick,' Sassy said. How right she was! Brown Owl took him to a deck-chair in a sheltered place and had to pick him up to put him on to it.

But although it was not a very cold night, Sam was shivering, so Amanda, who felt perfectly warm, put her jersey over him, too. If only he could have been seasick peacefully! But no. When he was not being seasick, he cried and he yelled and called for his mother, which was even worse.

Of course everybody was very sorry for him, and all the Brownies grinned like anything to show how Brownies smile whatever happens. The only Brownie who was not smiling was Sassy, and for once she was not at all pleased with her twin.

'He ran away and left me, and I got lost by the castle,' she said. 'And it's not fair. He's a very naughty boy.'

The sea got rougher and rougher, and more and more people were being seasick, but Sam was not being seasick any more. He just cried and went on making a terrible fuss about the dreadful headache he had.

'It's no good everybody trying to nurse him,' Brown Owl said. 'Tawny will take you on tour of the boat, and I'll stay with Sam.'

Walking about was great fun! The Brownies laughed so much as they tried to go along without holding on to anything. It was getting dark now, and lights began to appear on deck where the awnings had been put up to protect the passengers from the spray. There was still one place where the Brownies could go for a good splashing. It was while they were standing there that they first saw the little flicker of lights in the distance that showed that home and England were not so very far away.

'I never knew England looked so pretty,' said Sassy.

'That's because we can only see a little bit of it,' Jeanie explained. 'Because of the world being round.' Sassy found this very difficult to understand.

Gradually as they drew nearer to the land the waves changed from being enormous hills and valleys to choppy little furrows, which made the boat just as rocky but in a different way. Next time they passed Sam, instead of looking pale green his face looked bright red. It was Sassy who noticed the difference.

'O-oh, look at Sammy!' she exclaimed.

Brown Owl, who had been standing just behind him, peered round the edge of the deck-chair to look at him again. All the Brownies crowded round.

'He's all spotty!' exclaimed Sassy. 'He's got the measles!'

'You're perfectly right, Sassy,' said Brown Owl. 'I'm afraid that's what he has got. It's not sea-sickness at all. It's measles.'

'I told you I wasn't being seasick,' Sam grunted. 'I told you I wouldn't be seasick, even if I didn't have any pills.'

'Oh, dear,' groaned Brown Owl. 'Now all the Brownies who haven't had it will catch it from Sam, and probably all the children on this boat as well.'

'I haven't had it,' said Sassy, 'but I don't mind a bit now if I do have it, now I've been to France.'

'Shall we tell the captain?' suggested Jeanie. 'Then everyone who has been near Sam will know what will happen to them.'

'No,' said Brown Owl, 'I don't think that would be kind at all. It would only ruin their day out. Hardly anybody's been near Sam except you Brownies.'

The boat slid into the harbour and soon she was being tied up again. Down went the gangway and off went all the passengers. Last to come off was Brown Owl, half-carrying and half-leading Sam, who said he felt too weak at the knees to walk by himself. Brown Owl and Tawny made a carrying-chair for him with crossed hands. Brownies went in front and Brownies went behind to protect any new children who had not already been near Sam, from getting measles, too.

The first train was waiting for them in the

station, and Brown Owl carefully chose a coach without anybody in it. The Brownies all climbed in, very tired by now. Almost before the train had started, half of them had fallen asleep. Amanda was one of the few who was completely awake when it was time to change stations. She and Brown Owl and Tawny went round trying to wake up the sleeping Brownies, but some of them would not wake, and nor would Sam. He was sound asleep. So now the train had to wait while Brown Owl and Tawny and a very old porter picked up the sleeping

Brownies. They carried them out on to the platform, where they laid them down like parcels while they went back for more. Some of the Brownies had just woken up enough to stumble sleepily out. When the next train came in, the sleepiest Brownies had to be picked up and carried into it. Sam hardly stirred at all, but on the last lap of the journey most of the Brownies woke up and were more lively than they had been at almost any time during the day. It had been such a wonderful day, and if only Sam had managed to stay at home, it would have been perfect. The train came into the station, and there were all the parents waiting – all the parents except Sassy's and Sam's.

'I expect they're out looking for Sam,' suggested Jeanie. 'Poor things, they must be worried.'

But the twins' mother came panting up the station path, just as the last of the Brownies had got out of the train with the last of the bags. What was so surprising was that she had not even missed Sam.

'Well, whatever are you doing with this lot!' she exclaimed when she saw Sam leaning against Brown Owl. 'And speckled all over with the measles, too! Oh, what a silly boy you are!'

'Where did you think he was?' asked Brown Owl.

'Oh, he often goes out in the woods all day, and makes himself a fire and cooks himself his food, and we don't worry about him,' his mother said, giving him a good shake. 'Come along, Sam, pull yourself together. We've all had the measles up our place and there's no need to make a fuss. All except Sassy,' she said, and gave her a searching look. 'Oh, well, she'll get it next.'

A kind father gave the twins and their mother a lift home, so that Sam would not have to walk, although his mother was sure it would do him no harm and might even cool him off.

There was such a noise on the platform as all the Brownies tried to tell their parents everything that had happened to them. And then Harry arrived, and they had to tell their story all over again.

'There were sweets made like pebbles!'

'There were pebbles like sweets, and bread miles long. Look, we've got some!'

'And we've got smelly cheese and a little glass windmill, and postcards, and heaps and heaps of things for our French Day tomorrow.'

'I should think you'll all be much too tired for our French Day,' Brown Owl suggested. But there were cries of 'No, we won't!'

12 · French Day at last

Sure enough, the next day at twelve o'clock all the Brownies turned up at the Brownie Barn. They looked as fresh as though they had spent the day before in bed, instead of being on the greatest journey in their lives.

They were all carrying something for the French Day that they had brought back from France. Lucinda brought some beautiful pink cakes in a very French-looking cake box. Tulip brought a chocolate donkey, and Trixie a white chocolate lobster. Jeanie brought some lovely seaweed and shells she had picked up on the shore to decorate the edge of Harry's pool with. Trixie brought some mussels that her mother had cooked as soon as she arrived back from France the night before. Olivia brought some cheese all covered with grape pips to keep it fresh. Amanda brought some creamy French butter. Other Brownies brought long loaves and French potted meat and lollipops on sticks with wonderful flowerpatterns and faces woven into them. And last to arrive was Sassy, with two cooked French snails.

'How will you divide them up among so many people?' Lucinda wanted to know.

'I'll give them the teeniest, weeniest taste each,' Sassy said. Some of the Brownies came and sniffed them, and said not to bother about their having tastes. A sniff told them what they would taste like inside their shells.

'Hasn't anybody brought frogs' legs?' Harry asked, when he came to help them to put up a tent for the brothers and sisters to change in when they bathed.

'We tried to,' said Tulip, 'but they cost too much.'

'I got my snails cheap,' Sassy explained. 'Because they were rather old.'

The Brownies helped Harry to make his tent look very French by giving it extra high poles (found in the wood). Then they spread out the bottom like a kind of skirt, as they had seen at Dieppe. Amanda and Olivia fixed up a rope between two trees as a drying-line for hanging wet bathing-suits and towels on after the 'French swimming lessons'. Lucinda and Jeanie helped Tawny to make a camp-fire and light it and put a big kettle of water on for tea for the mothers when they came. Several Brownies helped Brown Owl to put a table out not far from Harry's pool, and to spread out all the good French food on it, with rugs on the grass nearby for people to sit on.

And then the mothers and brothers and sisters and friends of the Pack, including Mary and Cherry and Pat in Guide uniform, started to arrive.

Amanda watched them coming up the path. Last of all came the twins' mother, pushing her pram and, to everybody's surprise, some of her children were pulling another kind of a pram behind them with one of the babies inside it.

'Isn't it lovely?' Sassy said proudly.

'But what is it? It isn't exactly a pram,' Amanda said in a puzzled voice.

'It's a "pull-pram",' Sassy said. 'And Sam made it. Don't you see what it was once?'

But nobody did. The Brownies standing near her shook their heads.

'It's the side-car from the bicycle combination,' she said excitedly. 'And Sam took it to bits and put another wheel on, and now the babies like going in it better than in their other pram.'

Amanda smiled. Sometimes Sam really could be quite helpful in the end. But, of course, the only 'friend of the Pack' ('if you could call him a friend,' Lucinda said, till she saw the new pram he had made) who was missing, was Sam. Poor Sam was at home in bed, and his father had stayed at home, too, to look after him.

Everybody was very interested to see all the things the Brownies had brought back from France, lots of which they would soon be eating. When they had all had a good look, the mothers put the things they had brought for the party on the table, too – salads and hard-boiled eggs and milk and ice-cream – and then everybody sat down and the Brownies handed round all the good things and the picnic began.

Anybody who knew any French, talked in it, especially the Brownies who had been to France, and

discovered that it was perfectly French to call 'tea', '*thé*', and 'jelly', '*jellé*' and a café, a '*café*'.

'The little sisters may go when they're Brownies,' said Tulip.

'But not the little brothers,' Lucinda said firmly.

A little brother rudely put out his tongue at her.

'It's not fair,' he said crossly.

When the picnic had been cleared away all the children played French Tag till there had been long enough after the meal to start the swimming lessons.

Some of the little brothers and sisters had brought swimming things, and some had to borrow them from Brown Owl who had some extra ones. Some of the Brownies helped them to undress in the tent, and then all the Brownies undressed themselves and the swimming lessons began. They were great fun and there was lots of splashing and laughing. As it was such a lovely hot day, even the smallest babies wanted to get wet, so Harry made a nice clean place for them in the stream where they could paddle or sit or splash.

Then it was time for tea. Harry said it was not a very French thing to have, but *some* French people had it, and the kettle was boiling and there was still plenty left to eat, so they might as well.

When nearly all of the French food had been eaten and everybody had had a wonderful time, Amanda's mother got up and said that she wanted to make a speech. Everybody clapped. Luckily the speech was not very long, and it was mostly about Brown Owl and Tawny, and how clever they were to get the Brownies to do such interesting things.

'I don't suppose there is another Brownie Pack in England that's been to France for the day, as well as bringing someone back with measles,' she said, and everybody cheered. 'And what's so nice is that all the Brownies go on helping everybody else, even when they're not doing exciting and unusual things with Brown Owl and Tawny. It's a good thing, and we like it.'

Brown Owl made a speech, too. She said that the Pack couldn't do exciting and unusual things if it were not for the parents being so brave letting them do them!

Then Tawny got up and said that she was not going to make a speech, but that Harry had something to say that might interest a few people.

All the Brownies helped Harry to stand up, and gave him an extra push so that he could be heard better. 'It's not fair that the girls should have all the fun in this village,' he said, 'or be the only ones to learn to be useful and to give helpful parties like this. I can think of at least one boy who would like to do it, too.'

Now everybody cheered and laughed, because they all knew that he was thinking about poor Sam in bed.

'And my sister and Brown Owl knew it wasn't fair, too,' he went on, 'so they pushed me off for some training. Now, in case anybody wants to join, we're starting Cubs and Scouts in the village.'

The roar from the boys was only drowned by the squeaks of excitement from the Brownies, and all the parents there thought this was a wonderful idea. If the Brownies had not been surrounding Harry, he might have been knocked over by all the boys who rushed to tell him they wanted to be Cubs.

The French party ended, and the Brownies stayed behind to clear everything away and then followed their families home. But Amanda walked slowly home with Sassy.

'Do you think Sam will want to join?' Amanda asked anxiously.

Sassy smiled, and all her freckles seemed to get pushed together as she said:

'Of course Sam's going to be a Cub! *He* thought of it! It was Sam who went to Harry and said if somebody didn't start Cub's soon, he'd think of a way of joining the Brownies.'

'Then that's all right,' said Amanda, with a big sigh of relief. 'Look, here's some French pebbles to take to Sam, and a bag of mirabelles.'

They said good night, and Sassy went into her house and Amanda set off across the fields to the farm.

Knight has a whole range of paperbacks for boys and girls, from mystery, adventure and crime to fantasy, animal stories and factual books on sport and other activities for the holidays.

If you have enjoyed THE BROWNIES' DAY ABROAD, you will like the other Knight Brownie books by Verily Anderson, which you will find on the following pages.

VERILY ANDERSON

The Brownies and their Animal Friends

Amanda and her Brownie Friends decide to
have an animal quest – and the results amaze
even Brown Owl. But the Brownies' love and
experience of animals is very useful when they
are asked to provide a special item of
entertainment at a festival. A festival which is
more exciting than anyone could have guessed.

VERILY ANDERSON

Brownie Cook Book

Lots of recipes for Brownies of any age. This
book has hints on helping in the kitchen and on
the tools you will need for your own cooking as
well as a step-by-step guide for making fish
cakes, shortbread, pancakes, meringues and
many other tempting dishes.

Other Brownie books from Knight by Verily Anderson

All these books are available at your local bookshop or newsagent, or can be ordered direct from the publisher. Just tick the titles you want and fill in the form below. Prices and availability subject to change without notice.

KNIGHT BOOKS, P.O. Box 11, Falmouth, Cornwall.

Please send cheque or postal order, and allow the following for postage and packing:

U.K. – One book 25p plus 10p per copy for each additional book ordered, up to a maximum of £1.05.

B.F.P.O. and EIRE – 25p for the first book plus 10p per copy for the next 8 books, thereafter 5p per book.

OTHER OVERSEAS CUSTOMERS – 40p for the first book and 12p per copy for each additional book.

Name..

Address ....

....